Marrying Her Highland Enemy

Duel

The Dowager's Son

Winning the Dukes Heart

By: Emma Atwell

Table of Contents

Marrying Her Highland

The Duel

The Dowager's Son

Winning the Dukes Heart

Marrying Her Highland Enemy

*****

1: Rhona's Plot

"Adair Campbell is a bloody murderer, Mother, and I won't marry him!" Rhona MacDonald of the Clan MacDonald threw down the summons letter on the rough wood table and folded her arms across her ample bosom. "You must be mad to have agreed to this! These people are our enemies!"

Her tiny, fragile mother cringed, and some of Rhona's anger faded from guilt. Rhona took after her lost father, Bran MacDonald, dead now for ten years—and as such, she and her mother Una were all but opposite in looks. Una was a pale-skinned blonde, waifish and nervous, her hair wavy and almost colorless, the gray mixing with the gold invisibly. Her eyes were a washed out blue-gray, and she clutched her tartan shawl around her at all times for security. But Rhona was tall, almost mannishly so, and robustly built, all curves and wiriness under her rough shift and apron. Her dark red hair fell in ringlets across her shoulders now; she had been brushing it out when her mother had brought the letter and told her what she had agreed to. The eyes that had blazed so just moments ago were the bright blue of a summer sky.

"Please, Rhona love, don't act like this. We need the marriage if we wish to have even a prayer of getting your father's lands back!"

"Lands the Campbells stole after burning us out!" Rhona seized the letter and skimmed it, feeling her stomach boil with rage as she read the summons once again. Her mother had agreed to it: she was to be packed off to Castle Stalker to marry a Campbell heir. "And here you are selling me off to them to get back what's rightfully ours! I'll have to lie down for a murderer and bear babies into that bloody-handed clan of king-kissing betrayers for the rest of my life!"

"Adair was not counted among the Campbell guests who betrayed us at Glencoe--"

"That matters not one bit—he's a bloody Campbell! Is ten years so long to you that you forgot what they did?" A decade ago, she and Una had stumbled from the burning ruins of Glencoe, then faced a month starving in a cave while clan-mates died around them from exposure, illness and lack of food. The Campbells had done this, responding to MacDonald hospitality by slaughtering them in their beds and burning their homes. Anything they had not ravaged they had taken for themselves. How could her mother's memory be so short?

Una burst into tears. Rhona stared at her for a long moment, then turned on her heel and stalked outside, barely remembering to grab her shawl before she opened the door. *My own mother.*

The morning chill slapped her in the face, distracting her somewhat from her rage. She sighed and leaned heavily against the battered stone-and-timber wall beside the door. The hovel they shared was the only hospitality their cousins on Skye had been able to afford them. Sitting on the edge of a crofter cousin's acreage, it was a miserable little pile that Rhona kept up as best she could by herself. Una could cook, clean and mend, but was useless for heavier work. When it came time to clamber up to the roof to change the thatch, or gather wood for the fire, or work her cousin's land in trade for the food they needed, it all fell to Rhona. She felt her heart sink into her shoes. The refurbished mass of rocks and old timber behind her was nothing like the home she remembered, but it *was* home now, and had been for ten years.

But this afternoon, that would change. A host of Campbell men came from Castle Stalker for her, to bear her back with them for marriage to the Chief's aging son. And perhaps she would spend her time after that warm, and properly fed, and clothed in something besides five-times-repaired homespun and patched scraps of tartan. But she would also be a captive of the worst band of murderers in the Highlands.

Una would be there too, but she had chosen this. She had a knack for making nice with even the worse sorts of monsters, and apparently she imagined Rhona should do this as well. But Una did not have to marry one of them. She did not have to lie with one of them, and bear his babies, and wear the tartan of his filthy, dishonored clan instead of her own. No; that 'honor' she saved for her daughter, as she had every other bit of ugly and dangerous work that needed doing since their escape.

I should cast myself off a cliff into the sea. Then she'll have to whore herself out to the enemy instead.

She wiped a tear off her freckled cheeks impatiently. Unlike Una, whose blood seemed made of whey, Rhona had her father's mettle along with his looks. She knew that as hellish as the situation was, she would have to see it through. The host came to their hovel soon, and they would come armed. If she refused to give herself up, the Campbells would do what they did best, and they and their cousins would suffer.

Father, she thought desperately. *Una has betrayed us both. What should I do? They will strike your blessed name from me and force me to wear the Campbell plaid.* Tears blurred her vision. *If I kill myself to keep my honor they will take it out on our cousins. How do I escape this trap?*

The missive she had left crumpled on the table inside explained the depths of Una's betrayal. Supposedly, James Campbell, Adair's father, believed that intermarriage would help to end the feud between their clans. That was the sweetened lie he had passed to Una, and she had swallowed it and volunteered her barely-of-age daughter for the venture. She had then kept it from Rhona for the whole of a month, skulking around, hiding the letters, hiding her own fate from her, so that she would have no chance to rebel. Una had finally told her a few minutes ago, and Rhona felt her stomach bind itself into a tiny, tight knot of burning pain as the horror of it sank in.

Inside, her mother was sobbing and wailing: in shame, Rhona hoped, though she doubted it. For years, she had tended her mother in her mourning. But years of sadness had curdled into moroseness and self-pity, until Una defended herself with tears every time Rhona grew impatient with her. *Please, Rhona. Please, I can't face this.* "You can't face anything," she growled bitterly as she pushed away from the wall and started walking up the hill to the low stone boundary fence. "You make me face it in your stead."

But it was done, and though she swore she might never speak to her mother again, her anger at that betraying cow couldn't take up her thoughts right now. She had to figure out what to do.

She reached the boundary fence and sat on it, smoothing her worn, colorless skirt across her thighs as she stared out over the moors beyond. She kept having to fight back tears. But slowly, as she watched the sheep wander the stubbled fields for their forage, an idea dawned on her.

She had a single sock-knife of her father's which she had carried with her from their burning home. Its good steel blade and tough bog oak grip had stood up to a decade of work and resharpening, and even now its weight in her sleeve reassured her. She couldn't do anything while they were near MacDonald land, but once they reached the castle, there was nothing stopping her from avenging herself *and* her father. No one ever expected a young girl to know a thing about using a knife; likely, they wouldn't even search her.

Perhaps instead of giving their son a wedding, I'll see to it they give him a funeral. Anger and determination gathered in her chest like hot iron. *Or perhaps I'll put this in his father's neck the moment he gets within reach. They'll kill me for it, but better death than belonging to them.*

She looked down the hill at the little hovel, at its narrow chimney and battered thatch, and remembered their cottage at Glencoe, warm and snug thanks to her father's loving labors to keep it in good repair. Her childhood had gone up in smoke that icy night, the burning town a pyre for dozens of her family members. *Mother, how did you convince yourself that selling me out to our enemies was somehow better than a home on the land of our own kinsmen?* It smelled of mildew when it rained; it was drafty, chilly, and gathered damp from their breath until it dripped off the roof beams. But....

She shook her head, and reached to squeeze the grip of her knife through the fabric of her sleeve. Her life was over, yes, thanks to her idiot mother. But she would strike one more blow for MacDonald before she went.

The day had grown passably warm and bright by the time four men rode up the path beyond the fence and made their way toward the hovel. Rhona stood with a small bundle of her belongings clutched to her chest, Una beside her with one of her own.

"You're not talking to me anymore, then?" Una mumbled at her as they watched the men approach.

"If you had any shame at all, you wouldn't even ask me that."

Una gulped and sniffled, but when she saw Rhona was ignoring her she wiped her eyes and stopped. "I suppose that's fair. You won't understand. You're too young. But the truth is the same. The chance to end the feud is more important than any one person's life."

"Then marry one of them yourself. You didn't even bother to ask me."

"You would never have agreed!"

"That is your problem." Rhona glared at her briefly before turning away again. "Never did I imagine that you would betray me like this." She went silent, watching coldly as the four tall men in the blue and green Campbell tartan rode into their small, muddy yard.

2: Declan's Host

The four men rode geldings of good stock, leading two more behind them: duns and dapples mostly, each one saddled and burdened with carry-sacks. Each man dressed like a soldier, claymores at their backs and blades hanging from their belts as well, their tartan cloaks flapping and their kilts hung with hard leather sporrans. Three were younger men, scruff-bearded from the road: two dark-haired, who might have been brothers, and one with a beard the color of split oak. They talked and joked among themselves as they approached.

The fourth man led them, and rode out front on his gray gelding, the wind tossing the cowlicks in his red-gold hair. He had sprigs of gray in the grizzle across his chin, and crow's feet at the corners of his soft blue eyes, and he kept quiet as the others chattered. Taller than the others, his shape lean and hard under his kilt and tunic, he turned his attention to the pair of them the moment he entered the yard. Perhaps that was why she noticed him most: his narrow, handsome face turned toward her curiously, while the others ignored them.

Curiosity turned to mild shock of some kind a moment after their eyes met; he stared at her, lips slightly parted, and then swallowed and dragged his eyes away to address her mother. "Una MacDonald?" he asked in a deep, soft voice.

"Aye, sir," she replied, stepping forward. "I was told to expect riders from Castle Stalker."

"We are they." He glanced Rhona's way again, and then harrumphed softly and lifted his chin. "Call me Declan. The lads and I didn't want to ride up on you with everyone. Gives a bit of a bad impression." The others chuckled briefly, and Rhona felt her cheeks burn.

True enough. None of us would accept a large host of Campbells on our lands ever again. But they don't have to laugh about it. She stared hard at their leader's face, not bothering to hide the anger in her eyes.

He caught sight of her expression and his smile faded. He coughed into his fist, then spoke up in a more businesslike tone. "Our company's camp lies just outside your cousin's lands. We shall have our luncheon there, and then start out. Stalker lies a hard five days' ride from here, but we'll do our best to ensure your comfort on the way."

Rhona snorted. *Our comfort? We're landless and in rags because of you Campbells, and you're pretending to care whether we're comfortable?* But she kept quiet, too aware of his mention of more soldiers just out of sight over the hill.

"Thank you, sir," Una said softly. Declan dismounted in one fluid motion, landing with a heavy thump of boots, and went to help her onto her horse.

Rhona saw this, and set her jaw, walking over to the other unclaimed horse. It danced a little, but she spoke to it soothingly and patted its side. *I'm not upset because of you, you big silly thing.* She grabbed the saddle—and there Declan was at her side, reaching for her.

"Let me just help you there--" he started.

Don't touch me. "I do not require it," she replied in a tight voice, moving away from his grip quickly.

He stepped back slightly, blinking, a strangely hurt and disappointed look on his face. "As you wish."

She glared back at him a moment, then set her jaw, knowing she couldn't give him the sharp end of her tongue. *My cousins will pay for it if I do.*

Her shoulder cracked audibly as she pulled herself up into the saddle, yanking her skirts out of the way. She heard a chuckle in front of her from the other men, and gritted her teeth, settling herself into the saddle and fixing the fall of her skirt for decency. More chuckling. She glared back at those smirking faces—

smirking except for Declan, who was staring at her with a worried look on his long face.

"Looks like MacDonald women have more in common with hunting dogs' bitches than with proper ladies," the brown-bearded one sneered. She wanted to spit at him.

"I must apologize for my daughter. We have lived here alone since she was small, and she has had no chance to learn proper manners." Una's voice came out a rapid, nervous stammer, and Rhona felt a flush of embarrassment and rage roll through her.

"That's not it at all, you betraying cow!" she snapped before she could stop herself. Una flinched, and the three roared with laughter, keeping up their comments, suggesting that

Declan throw her back before they got her home and she embarrassed him in front of the Chief.

Declan just stared at her. And slowly, his face darkened, and anger started to gleam in his eyes. But when she stared back defiantly, he turned, and suddenly showed the reason for his anger—which was not what she had expected. "Shut it!" he snapped at his men. They went silent at once, Brown Beard blinking in shock at him. Declan put his fists on his hips. "She'll be Chief's wife one day. Do you think she won't remember how you treat her now?"

He sighed, glancing at her again before turning back to his horse. He swung back into his saddle and looked around at them, his expression gone grim. "Let's shove off, then."

They rode into the gathering day, the Campbell men chattering, trading gossip and comments on the poverty of the

MacDonald lands. Declan spoke with them sometimes, and sometimes talked quietly with Una—conversations Rhona ignored completely, hating the sound of her mother's whining voice.

She grabbed her arm now and again as she rode, drawing what little reassurance she could from the lump beneath the fabric. Only by hanging onto her rage could she avoid bursting into tears. *Be strong. Do not let them see the pain they cause you. Do not give them even more of a chance to laugh at you.*

Around midday they reached the camp, which startled Rhona with its small size and simplicity. Declan had brought but a dozen men to retrieve her, and the sight of the rough circle around the firepit comforted her some. At least their low numbers meant she need not quite be as careful with her tongue as she had thought.

Good, because I'm tired of playing prim and silent.

Una needed help off her horse. Rhona swung down by herself and simply walked away from hers, leaving one of the soldiers to run up and grab the dun gelding's bridle. *Now that I know they can't massacre us again, at least today, should I simply keep walking into the woods?* She wanted to. She would die out in the forest with no woodsman skills, supplies or even a heavy cloak, but that was better than what waited for her at Stalker. But she noticed that same set of soft blue eyes always following her, and knew she wouldn't be able to get away. She went to warm herself near the fire pit instead.

Luncheon was spit-roast rabbit with some bread and cheese. Rhona chewed mechanically, sitting as far from the others as she dared. Now and again she noticed Una or Declan watching her. She would meet their gazes with a dead-eyed stare.

Una always looked away, paling and trembling. But Declan...Declan always got that same disappointed expression,

his kindly-looking eyes carrying a scrap of sadness in them that she didn't understand.

Finally, he came over to her, and sat a little nearby on a fallen log, his elbows on his knees. "Are you well, Miss?"

"It doesn't matter," she answered honestly. Why was he even asking her? It wasn't like any Campbell would care at all about how she was doing.

He folded his arms and shifted his weight, eyes narrowing speculatively. "Then you are *not* well."

She scoffed slightly, pain running claws down her heart. "Why would I be well?"

He blinked a few times. "As I understand it, most brides are excited at the prospect of being married, especially if it improves their condition."

She couldn't help it. She laughed. It was a loud, high sound of bitterness and anguish, hurting her throat as it poured out of

her, and stopping the conversations around the campfire for a few moments. Her mother was gesturing frantically at her to be

silent—which made her laugh a bit longer before she finally got the outburst under control.

"I'm sorry, did I say something funny?" he asked in a puzzled tone.

"Not funny. Ridiculous. You think I should be excited?" she hissed, lowering her voice. "I'm being married off to the Clan that murdered my father, burned us out of our homes and stole our lands. The idea that I would be *excited* about my coming imprisonment is completely laughable."

He sat back, eyes wide and startled, as if she had slapped his face. "You're not being imprisoned. It isn't like that--"

"How is it not like that?" she demanded, barely able to keep her voice down enough to avoid eavesdroppers. "I was only told this morning that I get to spend the rest of my life bearing babies for some bloody-handed Campbell who is twice my age, so my mother can enjoy eating full meals and sleeping warm again." Her vision blurred and she turned her face away, awkwardly wiping her eyes.

"Wait...." He sat there blinking at her, his face gone pale under the stubble and road dirt. "She didn't even...tell you...until today?" He looked over at Una, his expression shocked...and now, a little scandalized.

"No, of course not. She knows I would have run away or hung myself rather than face this otherwise."

"Hung yourself?" he looked horrified. She wondered what isolated tower he had been living in that her reaction was that much of a surprise. "Must I put a watch on you to keep you alive, then?"

"I suppose you'll be in trouble if you don't deliver your laird's victim to him," she muttered resentfully.

"Victim—girl, no one here or at Stalker plans to make a victim of you!"

"You already have," she spat in quiet rage. "I was barely eight when your people used our hospitality as a means to

murder us in our beds and burn out the survivors. I spent many nights huddled in a cave with the other survivors, watching

people around me die." She folded her arms, touching the lump in her sleeve for comfort.

He drew a shuddering breath. "The alliance is supposed to put an end to all that--"

"It won't. Not because we won't deal with *you* honorably— that's always been the MacDonald downfall—but because you

Campbells won't think twice about betraying us again if it's to your advantage." She mopped her eyes with her ragged sleeve.

"And you should have found a better way than forcing a survivor of your massacre to marry one of you!"

"It wasn't forced! Your mother was asked permission, honorably so--"

"None of you thought to ask *my* leave at all, did you?" She looked up at him, tears spilling down her cheeks, seeing the shock and worry on his face but taking it for an act. He was a

Campbell after all. They had no hearts. "I have to submit myself to this, or you'll likely take it out on the rest of MacDonald's survivors. And I will." *At least until I get this Adair in stabbing range.* "But don't expect me to pretend I am happy, or pretend

that I am bettering my situation. This is a nightmare for me, and no mistake."

"I...." he mumbled breathlessly. "I haven't the slightest idea what to say."

"Don't say anything, then. Just leave me alone."

He sat quiet for a little while, and then got up and walked back toward the knot of people sitting round the firepit. He sat where he could see her, and now and again she caught him

watching her as she sat silently weeping—and cursing herself for giving in to tears.

They buried the firepit and left soon after, starting a journey that was rough that not unbearable. Each day they spent long hours in the saddle, and sometimes the rain drizzled down

on them endlessly. After a few days, the bread had gone completely stale, and the last of the cheese was gone. Forage

turned up mushrooms, and the odd squirrel or coney, fortunately plump from late-fall fattening. It was something to fill her belly,

and Rhona took the rough meals and rough living without complaint.

Una tried to get Rhona to forgive her several times a day. She would ride up beside Rhona and try to talk to her. Rhona

squashed the twinges of guilt she felt and ignored her, even when Una started crying. If she looked like a cold bitch to the others,

so be it. Why spare kindness for the mother who had betrayed her?

Declan, on the other hand, simply looked after her. He would bring her food and water, he checked her horse for her, and now and again he spoke to her gently. He was so quiet and

unassuming in his approach that after a while, she almost started to look forward to their conversations.

"Why are you so cruel to your mother?" he asked her on the third afternoon, as they sheltered in a tight copse from a sudden, icy downpour.

"I am not cruel to her. I simply want nothing to do with her."

"But she is your mother," he said in that soft confusion.

She turned to look at him, standing there tiredly with rain in his hair. "No one who loved me would force me to suffer a fate such as this."

A hint of desperation entered his eyes. "Do you hate the whole of my clan so much, Rhona?"

"I do not hate *you*, Declan," she replied honestly, "But that is only because you of all of them have not been cruel to me. But it is not for the Campbells to tell any MacDonald to lay the feud aside and forgive you. Not when your lot has profited so from our suffering."

"You may well be right," he mused, startling her again. He was always shocking her: his kindness, his thoughtfulness. *They must have sent him because they knew he was good with people, and would not be as cruel as his kinsmen.* He looked up at her, with deep sadness. "I suppose you hate the Chief's son as well."

"He is the shackle they will put on me," she replied in a voice gone desolate. "He will take the place of any who might

have loved me, and shown me what happiness is like. How can I love a man of the enemy, who is forced on me? I do not hate him

personally, but every time I gaze upon his face, I will be reminded of my grief."

"Do you see no value, then, in ending the feud?" The frustration in his voice made her look at him sharply.

"I don't think it will end, even if I endure this marriage somehow. Your clan has shown they will betray anyone in the name of the King and their own gain. Why would my presence change any part of that?"

He stood silent beside her, and she realized after a moment that he had set himself between her and the wind, making a shelter of himself. He finally drew a deep breath and sighed. "Your mother believes you are being selfish."

She scoffed. "Selfish. Because I don't wish to have my entire life sacrificed for what she foolishly believes to be the greater good."

He swallowed, his face gone pale and lined with tension, as if she had insulted him personally with her rejection of the plan.

Or perhaps, of his clan-mate. "Have you thought perhaps that Adair himself was given no choice in the matter either?"

That startled her, and she looked back at him quietly for a few moments. "Perhaps then he feels some scrap of what I do. If so, perhaps he will understand why our marriage will be a thing I can barely endure." She let out a bitter laugh. "Or perhaps not. You seem the only Campbell with a heart, and even you don't understand."

"I wish to," he replied softly. He reached up, and one callused thumb brushed a tear off her cheek. His skin was warm, and his hand smelled of saddle-leather and wood smoke. She

lowered her head, fighting sobs, but she didn't pull away.

3: Bandits

That night as she readied for sleep she heard some of Declan's men talking around the dying firepit, and felt her blood start to boil.

"She's awfully cold and haughty for a ragamuffin like that. Does she plan to be married in that same dress, with mud at the hem and holes in the sleeves?" The unfamiliar voice barked with laughter, and a few others joined it. "She looks like someone dug her out of a midden."

"Eh, she might clean up well. She's young. Got a nice arse. Still don't know what Adair sees in her, though."

"She's the last MacDonald from the massacre to be of marrying age. Doesn't matter though—she'll be an ugly cow no matter how hard you scrub and how much lace and ribbons you throw on top." The voice gave a sharp, snarling laugh. "We should despoil her while he's gone, and force him to look elsewhere for a wife, for his own good."

"That's disgusting. Are we ravagers of women now?"

"That's not a woman, that's a MacDonald whore." She heard him spit.

Rhona stood, wrapping herself in the cloak Declan had loaned to her, and pulled her boots back on. There was only one response to a Campbell soldier proposing her rape, and that was

to get away as quickly as she could. Stomach fluttering in terror but teeth set, she felt for the knife in her sleeve and then looked

over at the stand of trees where the horses were tied. Guarded. Of course. *On foot, then.*

Without a word, and without looking to see if Una stirred from sleep or Declan had returned from gathering wood, Rhona set her feet away from the glow of the embers and started walking

into the forest. *If death takes me, so be it. I'll cut my own throat before I let any of those filth use me like that.*

Moonlight lanced through the tree branches, illuminating a deer path before her. She took that way for a while, knowing it would offer the best footing in the dark. No shouts rose behind

her. No one had noticed her leave, any more than they had noticed her listening. The Campbells held her in that much

disdain—all but Declan, the only one she regretted disappointing. The thought of his crestfallen face, and sadness in

his eyes, sent a twinge through her heart that she couldn't ignore. *I'm sorry,* she thought. *If I could only make you understand the*

horror of what I face, perhaps you could forgive me for making you look bad before your Chief.

But how could a man know this kind of suffering? *Father, I have never in my life wished I was born a boy until now. At least a man in an arranged marriage is going to be served and*

submitted to. He's just got no say in who it is that is serving him. Barely hardship, compared to doing the serving.

Her heart lightened a little as she kept walking, every step putting her further away from the Campbells and her conniving mother. *I will likely die out here, but I will die free.*

A branch broke to her left, and she swiveled her head to see a largish shape moving through the trees. *A bear?* She hurried

up, struggling along the deer path as brush started crackling behind her.

She heard a raspy chuckle—and knew she had been followed. She broke into a run, struggling to yank the knife from her sleeve. *No! No....*

A huge shape stepped out from behind a tree in front of her and grabbed her. She smelled unwashed skin and damp leather; rough hands gripped her arms and lifted her. "I've got 'er!" bellowed a gravelly voice. Then a sack was yanked over her head, and the world went dark.

She tried to fight, but every time she struggled a hard blow would rain down on her head or back, and leave her breathless and limp. Her ears rang. She felt herself lifted and carried, and eventually dropped near the heat of a campfire. She saw the flames' golden light through the sackcloth, and knew this was not the Campbells' camp. No. Someone else had her, someone with at least one accomplice—someone whose rough hands kept squeezing and rubbing her breasts through her clothes until she

was sore and sickened.

"Pretty little cow we've caught. Think she's a camp-
follower for the Campbells?"

"Looks like, ragged little thing. Suppose she's used to what

comes next, then." The second voice was already thick with lust;

she felt those rough hands slide under her skirt.

The knife. She thrashed and rolled over, crying out

wordlessly in pretend panic as she hid her arms from sight. She

yanked the knife free, slicing open her sleeve in the process,

and held it in her fist as the stranger laughed and forcibly rolled

her

back open. "Come on, girl, you know it'll go easier if you

don't squirm--"

She drove the knife toward the sound of the voice as hard as she could.

It struck home in meat: someone gagged. She heard shouts of horror as something warm and wet spilled onto her chest; she yanked the slippery knife free and the spill became a gout. She rolled free as he hit the ground, and slipped the knife under the edge of the bag, sawing at the rope that held it on.

"That bitch got Colin! Bring your dirk!" another voice roared in outrage.

The rope parted with a snap and she yanked off the bag—and saw two big men dressed in ragged motley bearing down on her with long knives. Hate rode in their eyes; she froze in spite of herself. She barely managed to heave herself out of the way when the first of them drove his knife downward.

A roar of outrage startled all three of them; the two men looked up—and then turned, one of them cursing worriedly under his breath. She rolled onto her back and looked—and saw

Declan leaping the small fire with his claymore out, eyes wild with rage.

He swung the massive sword so hard that it cleaved one man's head from his shoulders and bit deep into a tree trunk. Not

bothering to yank it free, he pulled his dirk from his belt and closed with the other man, who cursed in shock but fought back.

Declan barely seemed to notice. Blind with fury, he slapped aside the other's blade and drove his own into his chest.

The man's eyes went huge; blood gurgled from between his lip black in the moonlight. He fell to his knees, dirk slipping

from between his fingers and thumping to the ground a moment before he did.

Declan didn't bother to catch his breath before he crouched at her side. He stared in horror at the blood on her. "Rhona! Are you hurt?"

She shook her head as she struggled for her voice. "Not my blood," she managed finally.

He immediately grabbed a bandit's water skin to rinse the sticky horror from her bodice, still panting for air. The wildness was leaving his eyes, exposing the grief and confusion beneath. "Why did you run away?" he gasped out finally.

"Two of your men talked of raping me, so I would be despoiled and unsuitable for the Chief's son." She stared back at him defiantly. "You weren't there. So they planned to take advantage. I left before they could."

"Who...?" His eyes had gone round with horror.

She shook her head, pulling the cloth away from her chest and squeezing it out as he poured the water. The black blood slowly thinned to a dark stain. "I only heard their voices. I was not about to draw their attention by coming closer for a look."

His eyes narrowed as he kept helping her clean blood off her clothes. "I'll find out who soon enough," he growled, and his voice shook with so much rage that she stared up at him in shock. "We'll go back as soon as you're cleaned up, and I'll discover who planned to use you so foully."

Her face crumpled. "Don't take me back there," she begged suddenly. There was a limit inside of her, and she had just reached it. "Declan, please, if you have any thought for me at all,

don't take me back and let me be traded like chattel to your clan. Better that you kill me out here, so I can die free!"

He froze, his jaw dropping as she started to sob. "I have to take you back," he mumbled breathlessly. "There's no chance to end this feud without--"

She stared up at him bleakly. Then, without a word, she set her father's knife against her own throat.

"No!" He seized her arm immediately, prying it away from her body and trying to get the grip of the blade free of her fingers. She fought hard, but he was too strong. The knife slipped from

her grasp, and she was left sobbing as she hung from his grip. He stared down at her—and then pulled her into his arms.

She collapsed against him, smelling his sweat and feeling the rapid, hard thud of his heartbeat. He rocked her, nose buried in her hair, while she clutched the front of his tunic and sobbed.

Comfort. Safety. She didn't know how he managed to offer them within the simple shelter of his arms, but as the heat of his

body sank into her, she slowly felt her terror and pain drain away. She couldn't really hear his whispered pleas and endearments over the pounding of her heart, but she slowly calmed, until she relaxed against him.

He drew back enough to look down at her, and she saw a strange light in his eyes. Without a word, he lifted her, and bore her away from the carnage, over to the far side of the campfire, where the bandits' rude bedrolls lay. He found the cleanest and settled her onto it—and then crouched down over her, running one hand back through her tangled hair.

He struggled to speak, his eyes tracking around as if he sought out the right words in the air around him, but found nothing he could use. Finally, he leaned down instead, and pressed his lips to hers.

Warmth spilled through her, sudden and shocking; she gave a small whimper of surprise, her fingers still buried in the front of his tunic. She felt him shudder over her, and realized suddenly what lay at the heart of his kindness to her. It had nothing to do with duty—and everything to do with the stunned look he had given when he had first laid eyes on her.

No wonder he was so hurt by my anger at his clan, she thought. She had no idea what to say about it. Instead, she let herself respond, as she shyly slid her hands up over his shoulders.

The fire burned low as he explored her, breath shivering against her cheek as he kissed her again and again. His hands soothed her breasts where the bandit had left trails of pain; then his mouth covered them in kisses, leaving her squirming and gasping. His skin was smooth under his tunic, lean muscle rippling under her exploring fingers. His body trembled as she grew bolder, pressing against him and running her hands over his rump. When his hand slid under her skirts to push the cloth aside, she welcomed its warm slide over her skin—but felt stunned as well, and a little fearful, as his caresses woke a strange hunger deep in her belly.

By the time he dragged his cloak over them and pulled up his kilt, they were both panting and trembling, their mouths

rough on each other's and low groans vibrating Declan's chest. She felt something hot and sleek stab against her thigh, and

swallowed, closing her eyes as he parted her legs further with his hands. One of her cousins had told her a little of what shape

men's desires took when they brought a woman to their beds, and she braced herself for pain. But instead, he started doing

something with his hand between her legs—and she started shaking under him. Her mind swam, her throat tightening and her breathing gone to erratic sips as the hunger inside of her grew stronger and stronger. The world started to collapse inward, until

it held only him, and the strange fire his stroking hand conjured in her body.

Finally, she sobbed and lifted her hips—and felt something hot and firm slide into her, unfamiliar, the sensation so strong it did edge on pain. He moaned her name and started moving against her, in rhythm with the hand between her thighs. She buried her gasps in his shoulder—and then arched against him and sobbed as the core of heat and hunger inside her unraveled in waves of pleasure.

He kept at her, riding against her harder and faster, until his voice crested in hoarse little shouts and he went rigid. His hips ground against hers, slow and rough...and then he shuddered a last time and settled over her.

Declan, she thought, floating back to earth with a strange, tender bliss running all through her. She held him as he gasped for air, and smiled contentedly as she closed her eyes. The horrors from before seemed to fade like a dream, and she felt a faint glimmer of hope inside of her. Whatever else happened, at least now she would live having known the touch of a man who loved her.

4: The Devil's Staircase

"My father never led us into the raid against MacDonald at Glencoe," Declan said softly as they walked back down the deer path together. He held her hand gently, as if reluctant to stop touching her after their explosive tryst. She did her best to follow his explanation, her head still light with unexpected bliss.

"The law says a man is accountable if he should be ordered by his superior to commit atrocity and go through with it. My father and I knew that we could not carry out our orders in good conscience—but neither could we openly question my uncle, the Chief at the time. Do you know the old road known as the Devil's Staircase?"

"Aye, I know it."

"Our divisions were supposed to ride down the Staircase and cut off those who escaped the fire. And we did ride down the

Staircase—but my father and I went late to the battle, deliberately. We let the women and children and the few wounded men slip past us, and blamed the weather for the delay." He licked his lips, and slid an arm around her shoulders.

"My uncle choked on his dinner a few years later, and my father became Chief." He watched her face, smiling faintly as the realization dawned on her. "As one of the few who had not ridden against MacDonald, he was the only Chief we could have who was not tainted by the scandal. But that left the mess my uncle had left behind."

She blinked at him slowly. *This...this man is Adair Campbell? This man who loved me in my rags and ruin, and sought only to please me as I cursed him?*

"I had lost my wife some years ago, and after he was able to deal with the financial ruin my uncle had left us in, my father called on me to marry again. I was not happy with his decision, but I chose to obey." He gave her a sad smile. "But that changed when I first saw you."

"I... had no idea who you were."

"I didn't want you to know at first, for I knew right away that if you knew who I was, you would hate me at first sight. You are so angry over the arrangement that I feared I might never touch your heart."

She was glad he could not see her blush in the moonlight. "Well, you've managed it regardless, though I'm still mightily confused."

"Just...tell me you will give me a chance to show me that this is not a death sentence for you." The note of pleading in his voice melted her heart. Yes, he was perhaps twice her age. Yes, he was heir to the Campbell chiefdom. But he and his father had refused to take part in the massacre that had claimed so many of her kinsmen's lives. And his refusal had spared the lives of the escapees...including her own.

"I will," she replied softly, and he smiled with relief.

"I wish to know, which one of you fools decided it would be a clever idea to discuss raping my betrothed." Adair stood before the firepit with his arms folded, his sleepy, half-dressed men blinking at him in a knot by the bedrolls. "If he steps forward I will merely have him whipped. If he does not step forward, I will answer the insult by having him gelded."

Rhona stood near him, wrapped in his cloak, no longer so scandalized at having the Campbell tartan on her person. Una hovered a little way away, staring between the two of them in confusion and worry.

Two men stepped forward almost convulsively: Brown Beard, and a wiry redhead she didn't recognize. They both were pale as whey in the firelight. "Sir, we meant no harm--"

"You meant no *harm*?" Adair stepped forward, face congested, and grabbed each of them by an ear before smacking their heads together. The pair reeled, one of them starting to bleed from the nose. "You were openly plotting to ravage the woman we came here to retrieve. *My* woman. And she heard, and ran off to avoid *you,* and went straight into the arms of some bandits. I had to rescue her." He looked between the two of them in disgust, and then gestured to the others. "I want those two under rotating guard until we return to Stalker. Then they go straight into the dungeons."

Three days later, the pair did, dragged off by armored guards as the company marched through the gates of the tall castle. It had been a muddy walk through the basin at low tide, and Rhona was glad to walk on dry land again. The loch water had started returning as their horses had mounted the grassy bank of the part-time island, and now that she looked back she saw an unbroken line of water between the castle and shore. *My new home,* she thought, and the idea did not horrify her any more.

That afternoon she had her first bath in over a week, and when she rose from it she found a servant had brought her a wedding gown of white linen and Campbell plaid. She wore it before the priest that evening, and to the feast afterward, where Adair introduced her around as proudly as if she had come from a Parisian castle. But under the dress, high on her leg, she tied a garter from a strip of her father's plaid, which served to hold his blade against her skin. She no longer wanted Adair's life, now

that he had offered his heart. But neither would she surrender her pride in her true kin.

She spoke quietly with her mother at the feast, calm enough now to tolerate her again. But soon enough, she left her

mother and the rest of them behind, as Adair took her hand and led her up the stairs to his tower room. There, in a round chamber

dominated by a massive curtained bed, she finally untied the makeshift garter as he shrugged out of his clothes, and

surreptitiously pushed cloth and knife under the bed. No point in alarming her new husband.

He kissed her lingeringly before tugging her after him onto the mass of furs and woolens. She followed smiling, and settled easily into his arms.

Tangled up together, trembling, misted with sweat in the cool of the room, they moved together slowly in the deep nest of his bedding. They rolled and twisted and ground together until their breath came only in sips; until their whispered words fell apart into low moans of pleasure. When finally, her body tensed and spasmed around his own, she cried out against his chest, and heard him muffling a long, panting groan into her hair. Spent, they lay back together, she curled against him as they struggled for breath.

She still did not know if their marriage would do a thing to heal the rift between MacDonald and Campbell. But at least now her father's noble blood would run in Campbell veins, and give some quality of honor to their power. At least, where it did not

already exist, as it did in her new husband's noble heart.

*****

The Duel

1: Trouble in the Marketplace

Elyne MacKintosh felt the hairs on the back of her neck stand up and dance as she walked through the Perth marketplace, heavy shawl wrapped around her against the morning chill. Figures in her clan tartan milled all around her, greeting each other, haggling over stacks of root vegetables, apples and wicker-caged chickens. The basket over her arm was half full of carrots and turnips, and a trio of plump, blushing apples; she had eaten her own, the taste still clinging to the backs of her teeth as she navigated the crowded square. She had barely finished it when she had noticed the man following her, the first glimpse of his tall, perpetually scowling, pale-haired form robbing her market visit of its enjoyment all at once. *Not again,* she thought in desperation, and moved closer to her plump cousin Maeve as they looked over the remaining stalls.

"What is it, luv?" Maeve asked, her ruddy face collapsing into lines of worry as she caught sight of Elyne's expression. The two had the same coloring, red curls caught back with undyed ribbons and eyes as blue as the loch on a sunny day. There were differences, though: Elyne was small and slim, while Maeve was big and bluff, broad-shouldered and round-bellied like their shared grandfather. Elyne was pale to the point of looking almost fragile. Maeve was perpetually a little sunburnt from working alongside her crofter husband; today, she had left the tending of her own farmstall to him and her eldest so she could accompany Elyne around.

"It's that Englishman again," Elyne sighed. A knight, one who made it obvious from the fine cut of his clothes and the open carry of his long blade at his hip, the tall blond man had taken to following her through Perth whenever she visited town. One of the local signs of their occupiers' presence, he seemed to think he was entitled to whatever the town had to offer, taking what he wanted from the stalls against the protests of the crofters and merchants, threatening anyone who protested with a beating with the flat of his sword unless there were enough men around to scare him off. His gray eyes, which she had looked into all but once, were flat and cold as lake ice, and on the rare occasion that he did smile, it was cold and predatory and never warmed his icy gaze, not even a bit. He had set his sights on Elyne a month ago, and since then she had lived in stomach-jumping fear of the next time he accosted her. "He's after me again. And he looks even angrier than usual."

"He's probably heard about your betrothal," Maeve sighed back, glancing back over one shoulder to catch sight of him. "Bad enough that you should have to marry a MacPherson to keep them from squabbling us over Clan Chattan's headship. Now some gawky English brute thinks he has a claim on you too!"

"Oh, it's fine, Maeve, don't fuss. It's not just 'a MacPherson', it's *Donald.*" Which was awkward; they all knew the young laird, as Elyne had been raised in his father's court as part of a hostage exchange meant to keep the peace. In the years before her breasts had grown, she had played and explored and squabbled with Donal, then a reedy boy with hair as black as an English window-frame. Now, he had grown big and burly as his father had, his hair licked now with dark brown when the sun touched it. But she still saw the boy in the man: her best friend in a youth far too rambunctious to be properly ladylike. Politics or not, she really could think of worse matches.

"I suppose that's true. Anyway, if we intermarry enough, the whole point of fighting over headship will become moot. No more trading our little ones back and forth to be raised by strangers. Suppose it's something to look forward to."

"That's it exactly. Besides, at least I know he's not a brute like Sir William." For a moment, she again contemplated the awkwardness of figuring out how to turn Donal, ever a brother in her head, into someone she could think of as a husband. Including associating him with all those grown-up things she barely knew of, but which had made Maeve blush and laugh when asked about it. Do *that* with a childhood friend she'd seen go through awkward adolescence, and had never even had a bit of a crush on? It seemed strange. But better that than whatever it was that cold, obsessed Sir William had planned for her.

"Is there anyone we can go to help scare him off?" Maeve if anything seemed even more worried than she. Perhaps because after over a dozen years of marriage, she knew far more about men's desires, and how they might be twisted in the heart of a cruel one.

"Lord Carson cares not one bit how his men abuse us, you know that." Elyne picked up the pace a little, Maeve huffing along behind her. "I've thinking perhaps I should start bringing a stout walking-stick when I come shopping."

"Clever idea, but you'll only ever be able to take him by surprise with it once. A length of wood's not much proof against a sword-wielding knight.". Maeve was frowning, her eyes tracking around thoughtfully as they stopped at a baker's stall to add a few round loaves to Elyne's basket. "I think this is likely a job for Donal, if he'll take it up."

"I have asked him. There's been no answer. I suppose he is being traditional, but I wish he wasn't." They were to be wed in a few days; Donal was supposed to keep his distance until then. With Elyne's father recovering from a fall off his horse, and her mother and brother busy tending to him and their household, she was forced to look elsewhere for her protection outside her home.

"I'd send my boy, but he's no match for the likes of Sir William."

"Though he'd insist that he was, if I know Graeme." Elyne smiled a little.

"Well, he's eleven. Boys that age haven't yet grown into their courage. You'll learn soon enough when you have one of your own and have to chase them off the cliff sides and keep them from trying to hunt boar with their playmates." Maeve's smile widened slightly despite the ghost-pale Englishman haunting them from several paces back; she was proud of her son, reckless or not.

But just as quickly, she sobered, and coughed into her fist. "So you already wrote to Donal about your unwanted suitor?"

"Oh yes, I sent him more than one letter asking his help, since Papa is laid up. But he never writes back. You know how terrible he is about such things. I just hope he got them."

"Oh, Connor's a bit of a drinker, but he always gets the messages delivered around here. I wouldn't worry about it overmuch, Donal will have gotten them if you sent them. And I can't imagine his not reading them."

"I do hope so. This is getting very troublesome." She glanced back. Sir William was gaining on them, pushing through the crowd with a determined set to his narrow jaw. "Not certain

I would call him a suitor. He seems more the sort to pay his court with a knife at one's bosom."

"I fear you may be right," Maeve said gravely. "Let's get finished and get back to the stall before he catches up. He's a bit of a coward, that one; he won't be troubling you if Brian and my boys are around too. He's the sort who thinks all women are harmless and all men are deadly."

Elyne swallowed and lowered her head. "Let's just go back to the stall now, Maeve. He's gaining, and after the last time he caught up with me, I'd rather go without a ball of butter for the week than deal with him again. I'm sure my mother and Papa would agree." Last time, he had seized her wrist so hard that it had left a bruise on her milk-pale skin that wrapped all the way around her slim forearm. It was just barely fading now. That had been the night she had written her third letter to Donal back in his keep, telling him of what Sir William had done and that she had been injured in the process. In the back of her head, she was starting to resent him. What had happened to her childhood friend, that he would now ignore her calls for help? *Tradition be damned. If this keeps up, I can't say I'll think much of him as a husband.*

Maeve set her jaw. "I'll send Graeme after the butter for you, dear." They clasped hands and turned to hurry through the market, changing direction so fast that she heard a little shout of surprised anger behind them. *Good.*

They ducked between two stalls and down an alley between the Inn and the stables, Elyne knocking over some rain barrels behind her as they passed. *Hurry.* She hated that she couldn't stop long enough to see where he was; the idea that he might have somehow run around the long way in the time it took for them to get to the end of the alleyway terrified her. But then she heard a grunt and a stumbling sound behind them, and knew he had not thought of anything so clever.

They could not run in the press of the crowd, which closed around them like an ocean as soon as they hurried out of the alleyway. Elyne looked around worriedly for someone who might help them keep ahead of the furious, obsessed Englishman behind them, but the street was full of bustling wives going about their business in gaggles, most smaller than Maeve. From the cries of pain and outrage behind them, Sir William had started shoving them out of the way entirely. Elyne started to tremble as she hurried ahead, Maeve breaking trail for them through the people ahead. "Maeve--" she started fearfully.

"It's alright, luv, the stall's just round this bend here." Maeve's voice shook a little bit.

"Good, because I think--"

Her voice rose to a startled shriek as a spindly hand gripped her hair suddenly from behind and yanked her backward. Heads turned, and the crowd scattered away from her—all except for

Maeve, who turned and went even redder at the sight of Sir William dragging her cousin toward him by the hair.

Elyne screamed and struggled, eyes tearing up from pain as she was hauled backward. She could smell his usual mix of unwashed sweat and lavender sachet rising up behind her; she heard his hissing breath at her ear. "Quiet, you little Scottish whore!" he snarled. "How dare you run away from me? Now come along like a good girl, it's high time you pay me back for trying to make a fool of me all these weeks. You belong to me!"

"Get off me, you madman!" She fought and squirmed while he yanked her hair brutally. In desperation, she stomped on his foot as hard as she could with her heel, then drove her elbow backward into his gut. He grunted and doubled over, clawing for her arm with his free hand to try and get her under control. She drove her elbow back into his teeth, hearing her sleeve tear but not caring. "Let me go!"

Then Maeve was bearing down on them with something dark in her hands. "Duck!" she shouted, and Elyne did as best she could with that monster gripping her hair. Water splashed on her, and she heard a heavy clunk as Maeve swung one of the ironbound stable-buckets into the side of his head.

He let go of her hair to grip his own face; she stumbled away from him, scalp throbbing but free. "You...." he spluttered, even as he reeled; Elyne ran around behind Maeve, who stood like a bulwark, chest heaving with rage.

"How...how *dare* you!" Sir William bellowed. He straightened, one hand to his temple, bleeding from one nostril, and put his hand on his sword. "I'll kill you, you fat bitch!"

"Run, Elyne," Maeve warned in a hard voice. "Run for the stall. Don't look back." The tiniest shake hid in the bottom of her tone, and Elyne knew she was preparing to take the sword-blow if it came down to it. Sobbing in horror, she turned to run obediently--

--and saw a familiar broad-shouldered shape run around the corner from the direction of Maeve's farmstall.

"Donal!" she called at the top of her lungs, voice full of desperation.

2: A Husband's Duty

The struggle behind her suddenly ceased; she glanced back and saw Sir William looking up in horror with his sword half out of its sheath. Then back to Donal, running full tilt toward them through a hastily-parting crowd, teeth gritted and rage darkening his strong features. He hadn't yet drawn the massive claymore strapped across his back, but charged forward regardless, dark hair bouncing on his shoulders and his pale green eyes wide and wild. "Get off those ladies now!" he roared, and she heard Sir William gasp out all his air and stumble backward.

Then Maeve was at her elbow, leading her aside quickly as Donal ran past them with the edge of his great kilt flapping from his shoulder. She turned, and saw Donal barely stop in time to keep from crashing into the Englishman, who now really was as pale as a ghost. "What in Hell did you think you were doing to my betrothed, you miserable English dog? Make yourself scarce now, or I'll send your head back to your Lord in a box!"

Elyne's jaw dropped. She had been shocked to see Donal at all after the non-response to her letters, but now here he was, and just in time. But the protective rage she saw on his face as he stared down the bullying knight made that shock feel like mild surprise. One of his hands was hooked back over his shoulder to grab the hilt of his claymore, and his shoulders heaved with his heavy breath.

"H-how *dare* you," Sir William finally managed after some whey-faced stammering. "I'll have you arrested for this assault!"

"Oh really. Care to tell me what you'll tell the Sherriff when he asks why you were trying to drag an innocent woman into an alleyway by the hair, like some filthy Norman gone a-raping? There are twenty witnesses here!"

"That woman is *mine*--" Sir William babbled irrationally, and put his hand back on his sword. But Donal merely stepped forward.

"I don't care if you *are* mad, and worthy of my pity. Clear that sheath and I'll take off your head."

She couldn't see Donal's eyes from the angle she watched him, but something in them made the crazed knight drop his hand away from his sword hilt with his eyes widening. "L-Lord Carson will hear of this! I'll have you dragged before him in irons!"

"Try it. I bloody well dare you. You know he's short-handed men right now. You lot are on foreign soil, and outnumbered a hundred to one for two days' ride in every direction. You'll find no rescue if you tangle with us." He took but a half-step forward, and watched Sir William stumble back several.

"That is *treason--*"

"No one here is sworn to your usurper king, you filth! Now clear off!" He lunged forward, his blade rasping as he drew the first hand-length from the leather. Sir William turned and ran. Nothing had comforted or satisfied Elyne quite so much in a long time as the sight of him stumbling away, his pale hair flapping behind him like a flag of surrender.

She sagged, bracing her hands on her knees and struggling for air. Maeve rubbed her back. She heard the rasp of the claymore being replaced, and then Donal walked over to them, boots crunching on the stony street.

"Is she all right?"

"She's mostly had a shock, but he pulled her hair pretty badly. Were you waiting up by the farmstall?"

"Yes, I was hoping to meet you. But then some ladies came running past saying there was a mad Englishman trying to kidnap one of the MacKintosh girls. I figured on it being her, since I don't know anyone else around here with that trouble right now." He heel-sat in front of Elyse. "Are y'all right, Lyss?"

The nickname from their childhood brought her back to herself; she looked up at him, and saw the worry on his long face. She pressed her lips together, eyes brimming, and had to swallow before answering. "I will be," she mumbled. "Though I almost wasn't."

"I know." The lightest touch to the side of her face; her lips trembled, and she looked down in a mix of consternation and gratitude.

"I didn't know if you would come," she whispered breathlessly.

"I always will," he replied in a much gentler tone. "Here, see, you've spilled your basket out. Let's just get everything back together."

The carrots and dropped apples could be washed, but she looked down ruefully at the ruined bread, sighing quietly. "We'll get you more," Maeve promised, patting her arm. "And a new hair ribbon, seems he pulled out the one you had."

"Did it fall in the dirt?" Donal straightened to look for it, peering around at the dusty street.

"No, that creature took it." Maeve looked far grimmer than Elyne was used to seeing. "I saw it clutched in his hand with a fistful of her hair as he ran."

"Why would he do that?" she asked incredulously, looking between them. Donal gave her a blank look and shook his head, but Maeve's lips twisted in disgust.

"Now and again you'll come across a man who goes mad in a certain way. Like love gone rotten—leading them to act like this. They'll steal things of yours to keep with them, because they're yours, because they want you and because a piece of you that they took against your will is the next best thing. My sister had one of those in her younger days, right after she lost her husband to the war. That sick little scab got caught stealing one of her chemises from the drying-line. And he was a proper Scotsman, not English at all! So it seems that this sort of madness can inflict itself on any sort of man."

"How...." Elyse finished putting the last of the dropped purchases back in her basket, leaving the ruined bread where it lay. "How did your sister get rid of him?"

"Oh, he tried to pull her onto his horse one evening when she went out to the well, and she stabbed him through the hand. We found him balled up around the wound, crying like a baby. The Laird sent him off to Skye to serve some function thereabouts, and we never saw him again."

Donal puffed out his cheeks in exasperation. "Last thing we need on the near eve of our wedding is a madman like that around—and one of our English occupiers, to boot. I'm doubling the guard at the ceremony."

Elyse sighed relief. "Thank you. I cannot feel safe with that creature at large. That's not even love gone rotten—it's covetousness. I'm a trinket for him to steal, like my hair ribbon." *Not much of a surprise. I've yet to see a single one of our occupiers who seems even capable of love, or kindness.*

He nodded, and straightened, bowing to them both. "Well, I shall lead you back to Maeve's stall, but then I must take my leave. Wouldn't be proper for me to keep too much company with my bride before the wedding." His eyes twinkled.

Elyse walked with them numbly, cradling her basket as she stared and Donal's back. Shocking enough that he'd grown up to the size of a warhorse, outstripping his father and brothers, but again and again she kept going back to what he had just done. His courage, and his anger on her behalf. How was she to reconcile this with her memories of the boy who had once stolen her ribbons himself? She remembered when he was shorter than she. She remembered his stupid pranks, the one time he had pushed her into a mud puddle and then cried when she had slapped him for ruining her shawl. Who was this strange, and strangely caring, man who had stepped up and taken that boy's place?

3: The Wedding

At supper that night, the carrots and turnips, soft from boiling, added some body to a thin mutton stew. She had kept the whole truth from her father, whom she knew would blame himself for being too injured still to look after her. But her mother had noticed her mussed hair and lack of ribbon, and so she had muttered a bit of the truth in her ear as they chopped vegetables together. "Sir William," she had said. "Donal and Maeve saved me. Don't tell Papa." And her mother had nodded grimly.

"Two more days," her mother, who looked like an older version of herself save less slender, said cheerfully over her bowl. "Are you excited?"

"I'll like being married, I think. At least I know Donal and his family, and his home." Safe behind the keep walls she had roamed as a child; she would at least never have to risk running into Sir William again.

"Aye, it's not a bad match." Her father sat sideways to the table, his bad leg propped on a stool. It tended to swell in bad weather, though the bone had healed and the stiffness was gradually going away. He could limp around with a walking-stick these days, and sit his horse again, but when it rained he was back to gritting his teeth over it and propping it up. He was a big man, still athletic at forty, though his time away from his lands had left him having to cut extra holes in his once-snug belt. His hair was a floppy medium brown, and his mustaches would trail into his stew if he wasn't careful with them. His soft brown eyes were the opposite of Sir William's ice-colored irises. "I'm just happy I'll be standing on my own two feet for it."

"You will at that, Papa, and I'm glad of it too. Though I admit I barely know what I am doing." She smoothed her skirts across her thighs nervously under the table.

He let out a little bark of a laugh. "That's how we all are before our weddings, don't you worry. You and Donal will sort it out. At least the two of you know each other. My ladylove here and I still had to get used to each other when we married."

"I suppose so. Though it's a bit of a jump for me. He was a boy when I knew him. The man he's become still seems quite strange to me."

"Oh, well then, I suppose that makes sense. But he's not so bad. I hear he's distinguished himself more than once in battle against bandits seeking to hole up on his lands. He's young yet, but he's growing fast into his father's boots."

She nodded and busied herself with a few bites of stew as she tried to imagine what being married to him would be like. She had asked both her mother and Maeve to explain a man's desires to her, and what to expect on her wedding night. But her mother had simply blushed and changed the subject...and what Maeve had said had simply not made all that much sense. *What is the use of that little thing he used to piddle out of? I've seen sheep and goats mate, but I don't know how people's bodies fit together, or what it feels like, or really what to expect at all. What is so troublesome to women about the subject that neither of them will give me a straight answer?*

It frightened her a little. She didn't know if it would hurt, or if it would please her as well as him; she didn't know if she would fall pregnant right away, or if it had to be done many times first. She didn't know whether Donal would even know what to do. He had matured slower than her, after all, and though he was fully a man now, it didn't mean he had somehow plucked knowledge of sex out of the air. Perhaps they would both end up fumbling cluelessly at each other on their wedding night.

Oh well. Better to be worried about that than about whatever it was that that beast of an Englishman intended.

Maeve helped out the last two days by doing Elyne's shopping for her, dropping off baskets at her door at the end of each afternoon. Elyne spent her last days at her family homestead finishing things she had promised to do and left off too long: mending, scrubbing, helping her mother and brothers replace the roofing-thatch. Now and again she found herself worrying that Sir William would think to come by; it was not well known that her father was injured, so hopefully his cowardice in the face of other men would keep him at bay. But when she caught sight of a figure on horseback at the edge of her father's lands now and again, dark-cloaked and without tartan, she worried, and wondered. Fortunately, whoever it was never came as far as crossing their property line.

Finally, her wedding day came; she wore her new chemise and tartan, her shawl and a new ribbon in the same forest green found in the MacKintosh plaid. The day blurred past and crawled by in turns; she could remember dressing, but not the ride to the MacPherson keep, nor what was said when she greeted her kin-to-be. She could remember the taste of the roast gamebird and mutton from her wedding feast, but not the oaths she took before the priest. And when at last she and Donal retired to their suite at the top of the keep's single tower, she found her heart in her throat, and her head too dizzy to let her do much besides put one foot before the other up the stairs.

"Are you all right? You haven't said a thing for a good hour." Donal looked at her a bit worriedly as he helped her up the last few.

She swallowed. Her legs felt wobbly, and the dizziness felt like it was getting worse. She realized belatedly what much of it was, besides the nerves of walking into a situation she knew nothing about: relief. Relief that after this night, she would be sleeping behind stone walls, and not wondering if that mad English knight might burst in on her in the dark of night to lay claim to her. She remembered the feel of his hard, clammy hand on her wrist, and shuddered. "It's all right. I just don't really know what I am doing right now."

"Ah, well, that's natural, I suppose." He scratched the back of his neck awkwardly and offered a small smile. "The wedding wasn't bad, at any rate. Think you could teach the servants your mother's way with mutton? I stuffed myself on it." He patted his belly, which was flat as a tabletop despite his claims.

That made her smile a little as they stepped up into the chamber. "I'll see to it. There's not an herb in it that wasn't grown local, so there's no need to trade with the English for their spices."

"Good. Last thing we need is to line their coffers with more tariffs." He sighed and unbuckled his sporran and sword-belt, pulling them off and setting them aside on a low table near the entrance. Elyse looked around quietly at the round room with its faded tapestries and heavily curtained bed, her hands clasped in front of her. Then he was stepping in front of her, reaching to take off her shawl and loosen her hair ribbon, and she blinked up at him nervously.

Not knowing what else to do, she helped him, and tried not to let the fear take over as he gently undressed her. She had hoped he would stop with her chemise, but as he started kissing her softly he nudged her back toward the bed, one hand sliding the cloth up over her thigh. The backs of her knees bumped against the edge of the bed; he reached down and took the hem of her chemise, then lifted the whole business off over her head.

She shivered in the sudden chill, blushing so hard she feared she might burst. But he stared at her with his chest heaving, and kissed her again, feverishly, and she felt him start to shake. Kissing him felt good; the slow, gentle pass of his hands over her flesh as he started exploring her sent tingles through her that cut gradually through her attack of nerves.

Slowly, she started to relax; finally her hands gained some courage the rest of her had yet to, and slid up his belly through his shirt. Timidly, she took hold of the pin keeping his tartan to his shoulder and unfastened it; he tossed it onto the dressing-table beside his sword, then unwrapped his kilt from around him, his breath gone shivery as he continued to stare at her. He bent down briefly to unfasten his boots and step out of them, then peel down his thick wool socks and kick them off.

When his shirt and kilt came off she stared at him as well, once again unable to reconcile the boy she knew with the burled and sinewed beast of a man who towered over her now. He had a few scars across his chest, long and thin, a little raised and shiny; sprigs of hair thickened down his belly into a dark thatch at his groin. And then there was the "little thing" she remembered from her youth, now not so little at all, standing up stiff and darkened with blood like an angry man's cheeks. It looked enormous, and she wondered what he planned to do to her with it.

He kissed her again, long and hungry, his hot breath shivering against her cheek as he climbed onto the bed with her. His hands slid down to cover her breasts and she gasped as his fingertips circled over her nipples. Fresh jolts of pleasure went through her, and she felt it down to her groin.

Time started to blur as he caressed her everywhere he could reach; her back, her legs, her buttocks and finally, the delta of her sex. His fingers explored her warm opening, and brushed suddenly against a spot at the very front that made her jolt and gasp. He smiled, and did it again. Then he gently laid her back, and set his mouth on her nipple as his fingers started to rub her there over and over again.

It felt so good that it made her feverish: she writhed under him, her breath coming out in low whimpers from a pleasure she hadn't imagined existed. Her hips started rocking against his hand by themselves; she couldn't seem to catch her breath. The intense sensations distracted her from his parting her thighs with his free hand; she arched and squirmed—and then felt that hard, hot length pushing into her, stretching open the place from which her courses came and sinking in fraction by slow fraction.

He went rigid as he entered, panting, his eyes enormous; a low groan tumbled from his lips, and then his hips met hers as he settled over her. He took his weight on his free hand, gasping for air like an exhausted horse as he started drawing his length out of her and then pushing it back in.

His hand moved in time to his sex as he entered and withdrew, entered and withdrew, again and again while he groaned and shuddered over her. It hurt a little, just a slight edge of pain around an expanding wash of pleasure. Her toes curled and kicked weakly against the bedding; her moans rose to join his—and then rise past his as a desperate need she had never known grew to match the pleasure. Was that her voice, begging him not to stop? Yes, it was. And bare moments later, she knew why—as a sudden unbearable wave of pleasure rolled through her, sending her up on her heels as she pressed desperately against him. The feeling washed through her again, again,

again...and then he pushed down hard into her and groaned hoarsely as long shivers ran through him.

He collapsed over her, his hand going still at her groin and then joining the other as his arms wrapped around her. She held him with arms and legs, eyes enormous as she stared at the underside of the carved wooden canopy. *So good,* she thought, astounded, even as her eyelids started to grow heavy. *It felt so good.*

She didn't realize that she had dropped off asleep until her eyes opened onto the blackness of night what must have been hours later. He had managed to climb off of her, and lay the covers over them both; she felt his smooth skin against hers as she curled against his side with one of his arms thrown over her.

As she stirred, he let out a little grunt, and rolled his head toward her. "Y'all right, Lyss?" he mumbled.

She smiled in the dark. "I'm fine," she said for the first time in months.

4: Ambush

They spent a blissful week together at the Keep, spending their days with Donal's family and touring his lands on horseback, and their nights in each other's arms. Elyse found herself hoping she wouldn't fall pregnant too soon, though if she didn't it would not be for lack of trying. She understood now why her questions to her mother and Maeve had been answered with blushes and giggling. She hoped that when the time came for her to explain the same to her future daughters, she would manage it. As it was, it took a few days before Donal finally admitted he had been given a talk by his uncle about the matter of sex, which had left them both red-eared but had left him with some idea of what to do. She wanted to do the same for her children, when they came. But she knew she'd still be blushing and giggling the same time, remembering what Donal did regularly to her, leaving her exhausted, wobbly-kneed and drunk on sensation.

But on the eighth morning, after their visit to the Keep's chapel, one of the servants brought her a folded note he claimed Connor had brought from Perth. She opened it and read the hard, square letters within, and went pale as Donal watched her.

"What is it?" he asked softly, eyes full of concern.

She slid the note to him, a lump in her throat. "I must go back," she murmured. "Papa's leg's taken a bad turn, and he's down with a fever. They don't know if he'll live beyond tomorrow."

He peered at the note, a strangely thoughtful frown on his lips. "Who wrote this, your uncle?"

"Must have been Maeve's husband Brian, my uncle can't write. It's not Papa's handwriting either, nor Maeve's." She looked at him pleadingly. "Can you come with me, Donal?"

"Lord Carson has summoned me to answer some of Sir William's complaints, or I gladly would. But I can only ride with you as far as town. I'll send guards with you to ride the last stretch to your father's lands."

She nodded, and reached over to squeeze his hand. "I hope he just needs tending. It's late in his healing for him to fall to a fever. Please join me there when you are done with Lord Carson."

He nodded. "I will." But his thoughtful frown never left his lips, and he folded the note up. "May I keep this?"

"Of course." She pushed aside her plate and stood, and he got up to embrace her. "I pray we shan't be apart long."

Once she was dressed and he had arranged for four of his men to accompany her, she rode out on the gray mare that had been part of his wedding gift to her, while he rode the matching stallion beside her. They talked now and again during their half-day's journey, and she felt again the tenderness that had grown in her toward him since he had first saved her from Sir William. By the time they parted company at the crossroads between

Perth and her father's lands, she felt her heart start to ache. She watched him and two of his guards ride away, and looked back many times when she started down the path to her family home.

The road ran like a stream between the rolling hills, looping this way and that, some of its turns drastic enough that she could not see beyond them. One of the guards rode a little ahead to scout these blind turns; the others stayed surrounding her, two beside and one behind. She felt her stomach start jumping a little as they drew near the border of her father's lands. *Please let him be all right,* she prayed as she kept on, trying to fake a calm expression for Donal's men that she did not feel at all.

They were rounding the last hill before her father's property line when the forward scout fell suddenly sideways, a crossbow bolt sunk into his neck up to the fletching. "Run!" one of the guards bellowed at her as they surged forward. But a host of dark-clad men poured suddenly over the hill, crossbows and long knives gleaming in their hands as they surrounded her and her remaining three protectors. She froze, the mare dancing fearfully under her. *Oh no.*

Sir William rode around the bend in the path, a gloating smirk on his colorless face. "Now then." he said cheerfully as he steered his bay horse toward her through the crowd. "Just the lady I wanted to see. I've a camp with a lovely tent set up just for the two of us, back perhaps a mile. I think it's high time that you and I had a nice, long...talk."

Soon after, she found herself tied to her horse, hands behind her back and her legs bound to the saddle. Blood itched as it dried on the rims of her nostrils; her face throbbed and her lip stung where Sir William's fist had split it. They had cut the throats of the three guards and left their bodies on the path; stolen their horses, and watched as William had "disciplined" her with one gauntleted fist. Aching, head still ringing from the blows, Elyse sat silent in her saddle, mind racing as she tried to figure out how she could possibly get away from this monster before he put his hands on her again.

The whole time they rode back toward the crossroads, he chattered on in the tone of someone reprimanding a small child. "I cannot believe that I had to go to so much trouble to bring you properly to heel. You Scots women don't have any idea how to behave. When your better desires you, you had best smile and go along, and do as we tell you. That is your place. You are *mine*. You were mine the moment I laid eyes on you and wanted you. That fool who thinks he is your husband? That miserable Papist? He's nothing. He runs off to Perth on a fool's errand. And even if he shows up, we'll shoot him so full of bolts he'll look like a hedgehog. Then who will save you? Your cripple of a father? I don't think so. He wouldn't dare."

On and on and on he rambled, tone gloating and pedantic, while Elyse's fists clenched and she wished he would fall off his horse so she could coax the mare into stomping him to death. But he clung to the back of his bay like a burr, and his mouth never closed.

What happens if we reach his camp outside town? What will he do to me? But she already had some idea, and her heart sank as they drew closer and closer to the crossroads. *Donal,* she thought in desperation, but chances were that he would take too long to realize that he had been caught by a hoax.

I will not cry. I will not let the tears fall. I will not let this wicked English madman see me in pain. She forced her chin up, forced her mouth into a line, looked at nothing as she rode, even as he spoke louder and louder to try and get her attention. Finally, his frustration peaked, and he suddenly back fisted her so hard that it knocked her half out of the saddle.

She felt herself sliding sideways against the ropes, seeing stars, head ringing again, but after the first breathless moment realized that the tension in the ropes binding her to the saddle had loosened with her shift in weight. She kicked the mare's side deliberately; the young horse reared, and she heard her chemise tear slightly as a rope burned its way down her thigh. The ground slammed into her shoulder and arm; she kicked again, and found herself free while her mare bolted haphazard into the crowd of men.

She got up and ran, hands still tied, clumsy, stumbling, while Sir William shouted behind her. She knew she had an even chance of getting a crossbow bolt to her back, but she didn't care anymore. *Better dead than in his hands.*

She made for a stand of trees just short of the crossroads, desperate to put something between herself and her pursuers. She could hear shouting and running feet behind her. But as she came close to the stand, she saw movement in the trees, and stumbled to a stop.

"Get down!" shouted a familiar man's voice, and she threw herself flat.

A storm of crossbow bolts burst from the trees, flying toward the men chasing her. Screams erupted; bodies fell. She rolled over to look back, and saw her captors retreating frantically, leaving a third of their number dead or wounded on the ground. Sir William had gone the color of moldy cheese and was struggling to control his rearing, terrified horse. He tried to shout orders to his remaining men, but the lot of them had taken to their heels and were running full tilt away, scattering in every direction.

Three tall figures rode from the copse she had sought shelter in, followed by two dozen more men on foot. Most of them had crossbows of their own, or the plain short bows local crofters used for their hunting. She saw both MacKintosh and

MacPherson plaids, and realized with a start that she was looking at her father, Donal, and Maeve's husband, all grim-faced and surrounded by people of both their clans. Maeve was there as well, shouldering her husband's crossbow while he rode forward with the other two toward Sir William.

"This is treason! How dare you interfere!" Sir William's voice had gone high and shriek with panic, pretending outrage even while his eyes showed as much of their whites as those of his horse.

"Sir William of York, I challenge you to a duel," Donal said solemnly in return. "You have sought to ravage my lawfully wedded wife, and done so through fraud by imitating your own Lord in correspondence." He held up a rolled letter with a scarlet wax seal. "According to this writ, he has washed his hands of you for impersonating him on official business, and we may dispose of you as we please. Dismount and draw your sword."

"Whu—wha—what? How? How did you find out?"

"I compared the letter you sent imitating Brian MacKintosh with that you sent when you pretended to be Lord Carson. The handwriting is identical. Truly, did you think that my wife and I do not talk?"

Maeve hurried up beside her and drew a long knife from her kirtle, using it to cut the ropes binding her wrists. Elyse sat up gasping, and Maeve hugged her tight. "There we go. You're safe now. He was never going to get back to his camp with you."

Elyse stared between her and Donal, who swung down off his horse and grimly drew his claymore. *He knew. He only took so long because he was gathering help.* Relief poured through her, and she let out a sob and laid her cheek against her cousin's chubby shoulder.

"Dismount and draw your sword," Donal said again, his voice terrifyingly calm.

"N-no," Sir William gasped out.

"I said, draw your sword." Donal still spoke in that calm voice, his claymore gleaming in his hand.

"*No!*" the dishonorable knight cried, and then wheeled his horse around and dug his spurs into the poor bay's sides. The horse bolted forward—and a crossbow bolt buried itself in the saddle leather just in front of Sir William's groin. He drew up immediately, gasping in horror.

"You have one chance to die with a scrap of honor, and that is to accept the challenge as given to you. Try to run again, and

Maeve here will shoot you in the back. Then your family can learn how you died running in fear from a crofter's wife."

Maeve smiled and straightened, lifting the crossbow—but Elyne stopped her as she stood. Battered and bruised, wrists stinging, arms aching, she still spoke up. "Give me the crossbow."

Maeve saw the look in her eyes and gave it up immediately. Elyse had handled a crossbow only a few times, mostly when her papa was wounded and teaching her to hunt gamebirds in his place. Sir William was a much bigger target. And the look on his face when she leveled the crossbow at him did her heart good.

"Elyse!" he cried out in a betrayed tone. "You wouldn't hurt me--"

She smiled slowly. "The first one will go in you arise if you run. I'm sure Donal's friends here will spare me their crossbows as well. I'll make you look like a hedgehog." She stared into his eyes, and watched him wilt under her gaze. "Now listen to my husband or I'll humiliate you to death."

Finally, reluctantly, he dismounted and drew his sword. She saw him shake; saw his lips tremble, and the mad, pleading glances he kept shooting to her. One of Donal's men led his horse aside, and he and her husband squared off.

She had seen duels before; they were gory and inglorious. But with the writ tucked into his belt, Donal could seek their vengeance freely, so for the first time, she looked forward to a duel's outcome.

Sir William screamed and charged her husband; Donal spun aside at the last moment and brought down his claymore once. Blood sprayed. A blond head rolled in the dirt. Sir William's body took a step, two, then fell to its knees and collapsed to the dust. It was over—in bare heartbeats.

A cheer went up from the Highland men; Maeve sighed relief, and Elyse smiled tremulously and handed back the crossbow. Donal handed his claymore off to one of his men for cleaning, and hurried to her side.

"I'm so sorry it took so long. I had to tell the Lord about William's fraud to gain leave to deal with him. He might not care what that beast did to you, but of course he would care about the misuse of his name." He brushed her bruised cheek with his fingertips, eyes full of concern—and she threw herself into his arms.

"It's all right. I know you did what had to be done. Please...please let's just get away from here."

That night the lot of them feasted on her mother's good roast mutton, bread from the marketplace and spiced greens.

They kept checking on her: Maeve, her husband, Elyse's parents, and Donal of course—who never left her side. She ached from her beating, but it would heal. William could never hurt her again.

"Well done, lad." Her father bonked Donal's shoulder with a fist, his eyes full of pride. "Knew we chose well. Give my regard to your family once you get her home, all right?"

Donal flashed a grin. "Aye, sir, I shall."

That night, MacKintosh and MacPherson broke bread together, talked and laughed, all rivalry forgotten for the moment as they celebrated a joint victory against an English threat. A hopeful sign—and more hopeful still, that even the English Lord had been forced to support their rights in this instance. Once the meal was done, she and her new husband held hands as the group traded songs and stories, going on until well past sundown. Tomorrow, they would ride for her new home, and celebrate in their marriage bed. But tonight was for victory, and a brighter future ahead.

******

The Dowager's Son

*****

1: Isabelle and the Harridan

Isabelle couldn't remember a time before her brief marriage when she had felt this particular sort of headache. It started at the corners of her jaws and radiated up to her temples, making her squint and her eyes water. She sat on the settee in the corner of her mother-in-law's parlor, a polite smile pasted on, her manner attentive. In the back of her head she congratulated herself on yet another convincing act; across from her in a throne-like parlor chair, her hostess yammered on, completely unaware of her daughter-in-law's deep desire to run screaming from the room.

"Now what I don't understand is why they would let some undereducated French girl play hostess at such an important public event. Her accent's so thick that I could barely understand her, she's got those typical horse-faced French looks that no one can stand to stare at for particularly long, and if you attempt to correct her behavior she cries and makes you look like a villain! Plus, they had all that inedible French food. Those smelly cheeses and that hard crusted bread I hate so much...."

Dowager Duchess Theodosia, widow to the late Duke of Kent, lounged awkwardly against her embroidered cushions, her body an overlong tangle of knees and elbows topped by a thin-lipped, ugly face. Her nose was roughly the size of a camel's, her eyes were the color of muddy water and her skin was as close to gray as a living person could come. She wore a garishly striped dress with a neckline that exposed too much of her hollow chest, and her voice was a deep, nasal bray that grated against the ears. Thin light brown hair clung greasily to her scalp in little curls, and she had plucked her eyebrows down to near-nonexistence, claiming haughtily that it was a "Renaissance" style.

Isabelle, wife to the Dowager's son and current Duke, simply smiled and nodded acknowledgment, knowing better than to try and actually address any of Theodosia's ramblings.

Whenever she had tried in the past, the gawky harridan across from her would simply make some snide remark about her

observations and continue yammering on. Rumor has it that the old Duke, who had died of fever a year ago, had given up the ghost

willingly so that he might not ever have to hear her non-stop ramblings again. But sadly, that meant that just two months into

her new marriage, Isabelle found herself trapped with the duty of being her constant listening ear.

Isabelle was nineteen, youngest daughter of a trader in exotic goods who owned a dozen ships and nearly as many London warehouses. Her father had achieved a peerage after

growing wealthy on Londoners' love of Chinoiserie, and had sought noble marriages for his daughters to secure his position.

Her eldest sister Fanny had managed the Duke of London; Isabelle had settled for a "lesser" Duke, but her relative lack of position wasn't exactly a problem to her. Not compared to the company she was forced to keep now, day after day after day.

She was an opposite to her mother-in-law in both personality and looks. Small, delicate-featured, with large blue eyes and jet-black hair tumbling in abundant curls from the crown of her head, she looked younger than she was. Normally quiet and studious, she spoke when she did in a soft, musical voice, her words thoughtful and carefully chosen. Her pale blue and cream dress, modestly cut, was typical of her style, and as always, she held a half-read book in her lap, which she occasionally glanced down at longingly as Theodosia yammered on.

David, I am not sure I will ever forgive you for forcing me to care for this crazed bundle of vanity and hate. Her husband the Duke was, as usual, absent. His usual habit was to leave on business early after breakfast, stay away for the remainder of the day, and then return for a late supper before spending the evening with her. Aside from his business concerns, which largely involved land deals within his purview, he had an assortment of obligations to the Crown and to the Navy, where he had served before his accession to his father's post. And when none of that served as an excuse to be away, he would plead social obligations. Whatever the current reason, it always resulted in his leaving Isabelle alone with her insufferable mother-in-law for most of the day.

"...I still don't understand why any upstanding member of British gentry would marry off their son to some French woman! She simply has no idea how to act in public! And then her idiot husband had the audacity to ask me to *leave* because *I* was making a scene? The nerve of that man! I have never been so offended. Someone should give him a primer on proper manners!"

Isabelle's headache intensified as she forced another polite smile. Part of the reason David had so many social obligations was that his mother kept damaging the family reputation with her habit of antagonizing literally every single person whom she came in contact with. It wasn't just that she was scandalously outspoken; that quality, the intellectually voracious Isabelle might have admired. It was the subjects upon which she chose to be outspoken that caused the problem: she expounded, not about art, or philosophy, or politics, or literature, or anything else which might have counted her among eccentric intellectuals like Isabelle and her own late mother. No; instead she chose to speak out in hatred and incessant complaint, feeling free to give her invariably negative assessment of everything and everyone around her.

"And really, I don't understand what David means when he says I am causing the family scandal. Just because a lady chooses to speak her mind in a polite and restrained fashion does not mean she is somehow a 'screeching harridan'." Her tone was so haughty that for a moment Isabelle's smile became a grimace as she fought another wave of pain. As usual, she was glad that she was expected not to speak through her mother-in-law's tirades, as she couldn't possibly have agreed with her assessment. Theodosia *was* a vicious, screeching harridan, and her constant complaining and attacks on people around her really *was* causing problems for the family reputation. As apparently, it had for years. Isabelle had sadly come to understand that the "social obligations" her new husband constantly spoke of largely consisted of apologizing for his mother's latest antics.

Isabelle's misery deepened with every week that went by without her husband doing something to spare her from his mother's constant demands for attention and sympathy. Theodosia's predatory attitude, her apparent dislike of everyone in the world except herself, and her open criticism of everyone she came across—including Isabelle and her own son—were enough to make even a much stronger person ill. Some days, like today, with a freak April snowstorm whiting out the windows and no chance of even a garden walk, she felt completely trapped. So much so that when she was finally allowed to beg off of further contact, she would weep, sometimes for hours. Her marriage might have conveyed an advantage to her father, and to any sons she might have, but for her, every day was now an insufferable chore, which did not end until the sun went down.

"Pay attention, girl!" Theodosia snapped, reddening, her colorless lips gathering spit at the corners of her mouth. "How dare you sit there daydreaming when you're supposed to be listening!"

A fresh surge of pain made her dizzy. "My apologies, Your Grace," she whispered in a strained voice.

"That's better." The gawky creature leaned forward, peering at her. "What's wrong with you?"

"I am ill, Your Grace," she mumbled. Her head was pounding so hard now that she was surprised her hostess could not hear it.

"Ugh! Well, get out of here! Stupid girl, you should have told me sooner. How dare you bring some contagion into my parlor!" Theodosia made a shooing-off gesture with one spindly hand, bony face twisting in disgust.

Isabelle didn't hesitate to take the opportunity once offered; she pushed herself up, clutching her book of poetry to her chest with trembling arms as she all but staggered out. She heard Theodosia scoff in disdainful amusement behind her, and then she was out the door and in the blessed solitude of the high-ceilinged hallway. The world spun around her, and she almost lost her breakfast. But instead, she managed to lean against the wall, breathing deep and slow until her queasiness abated and she could lift her head again.

"Horrible woman," she mumbled under her breath as she pushed away from the wall and made her slow, ginger way down to the far end of the hall, where her chambers waited. When she had first discovered her predicament, she had sent several pleading letters to her father, explaining that she was under constant torment from her mother-in-law's demands for attention and unrelenting, thoroughly-expressed hatred for everyone and everything in the world. He had written back reminding her of her "wifely duties" and assuring her that she would "get used to" her new position.

I have never thought of myself as the sort of woman who would come to despise the men closest to me. But my father has abandoned me to this for his personal gain, and my husband has abandoned me to this so that he need not deal with it any longer. May the good Lord give me strength.

Her legs gave out halfway down the hall, and she jolted to her knees, skirts puddling around her as cold tears spilled down her cheeks. Day after day after week after week, month by month, it felt that her very living soul was being sucked out her, by a woman with the personality of a gigantic tick. "Curse them all," she whispered, and muffled her sobs behind her small hands.

She heard footsteps and froze, expecting her mother-in-law to come up behind her and start showering her with mockery for her collapse. But after a few moments, someone settled a thick woolen shawl around her shoulders, and she felt a pair of hands grip them, gently and comfortingly. She looked up, eyes blurry with tears, and watched a round, red face and worried bright blue eyes come slowly into focus. Maeve, their cook and chief maid, a chubby, towheaded Irish widow who came like clockwork to announce every meal. She and Isabelle had never spoken before, and Isabelle stared up at her now, completely baffled.

"Oh, poor love. Has she worn you out again?" Maeve's voice with its soft brogue was filled with honest concern, prompting another flood of silent tears. "Yes, yes, I suppose that she has at that. Only a matter of time, really, just like with everyone." She offered both hands, and helped Isabelle up, her arms stronger than expected as she steadied the hapless teen.

Isabelle felt a faint surge of hope; until now, she had had no one to confide in who would actually listen. Her sister had dismissed her urgent letters as "whining", and the one time she had tried to tell her husband how she suffered, he had made some excuse regarding his business affairs and hurried out. She had grown unused to kindness; it caught her off guard. As the cook helped her down the hall to her chambers, thus, she finally choked out, "I thought everyone here was cruel."

"Oh no, dear." Maeve's smile was a tight line that didn't touch her eyes. "That's only Her Grace. Most of us are just busy staying out of her way, the Duke included."

"Yes, and then he leaves me at her mercy so he does not have to deal with her." Isabelle couldn't squash down her resentment anymore; it filled her tone as they reached her door and Maeve pushed it open for her.

Maeve frowned, but Isabelle could tell right away that it wasn't aimed at her. "I imagine he's too busy being relieved that he does not have to endure her any longer to give much thought to what doing so is doing to you, my Lady."

That brought fresh tears; she took out her handkerchief and did her best to wipe them away as she stumbled across the sitting room to her own window seat. The book dropped from her hands and Maeve retrieved it, worry deepening on her face. Isabelle practically fell onto the window seat, leaning her

throbbing head against the chilly panes in the hopes of easing it. "I cannot live like this," she confessed softly.

Maeve set the book beside her, and sighed, then dragged over a chair and settled into it. "There are many who have been in your position in this household, my Lady. She has driven off

servants who have attended this family for generations. She has no friends, so she seeks a captive audience to her complaints.

There's no one among the servants here who does not sympathize with you. Please, before you fall to despair, remember this."

"But what can you do?" Isabelle turned to her with pleading eyes, her lips trembling.

Maeve opened her mouth to reply, when a loud bellow echoed down the hall. "Maeve? Maeve! Where's my luncheon, you worthless potato-eater? It's three minutes past the hour!"

Maeve sighed and rose. "I've got to see to her plate. Should I bring yours here?"

"I don't know if I can eat. I don't wish to waste your good cooking."

Maeve looked at her with a sad, fond smile, and one chubby hand touched her shoulder again. "I'll leave it by the door."

"Maeeeeeeve!"

Another sigh. "Just remember, child. You are not as alone as you think. The Kent Duchy may have cruelty and selfishness in its blood, but most of the people here are not of that blood."

She stood and turned, hurrying out. "On my way, Mistress!" she called with all the fake cheer in the world.

Isabelle stared at the door after it had closed on her, and felt a strange mix of hope and bitterness that slowly gelled into determination. *If my husband will not help protect me from his mother's abuses, then perhaps I can gain the aid of the servants.* But for what? How could they possibly help, if they had no power at all within the household?

She was left wondering this as she sat there, waiting for the pain in her head to fade. When it did not, she retired to her day couch, drawing the shawl over herself and closing her eyes.

2: David

She woke when someone laid a hand on her shoulder, opening her eyes with a jolt of alarm, though the touch was gentle. Her husband bent over her, curly brown hair still askew from a day under his topper and his damp coat draped over his arm. He was tall and lean as his mother, but without her hideousness, having inherited his father's high-cheekbone, strong-jawed good looks and pale hazel eyes. Right now, he was frowning, a slight flush to his pale, smooth skin. She squinted up at him, bracing herself for disapproval that she had not endured the day's trials to completion.

David was a proud man, nearly as haughty in his own way as his mother, though nowhere near as cruel. When something was wrong, the Heavens would have to open before he would admit to it. Thus he had said nothing at his father's funeral; grieved not a bit at the loss of his brother to Napoleon's forces; and walked away rather than hear her cry about his mother's cruelty to her. She had tried to be patient with him; tried to love him regardless. But though their time in the marriage bed had been an unexpected treat, all she felt for him now when she looked up at him was resentment and a sense of betrayal.

"Maeve said you weren't well," he said in a tone that actually had a touch of worry in it.

"No," she murmured hoarsely, sitting up slowly. He had brought in her covered luncheon plate, and a cup of tea long gone cold; she reached for it regardless, her throat totally dry. A few swallows, and she tried speaking again. "I am... sapped of my health, my husband."

"I see." He brought and settled into the chair that Maeve had lately occupied, crossing his long legs and peering at her with that same thoughtful frown, as if she were a page in the family ledger that he was sorting out how to correct. "How are you unwell?"

"It is the same headache. But it grows less bearable by the day." She stared into his eyes. He *knew* what she meant, and she watched as he winced and looked away.

"Perhaps some of Maeve's herbals might be of help. I will ask her." His voice held hesitation at the bottom, and she cursed him silently for being so weak. But at least he was trying to do *something* for her, for once.

"If it will make this more bearable, I will welcome whatever concoction she brings." Her voice was a low sigh. "Where were you today?"

He went quiet. She always asked, and he often dodged the question. At first she had wondered if he had a mistress. But then his coachman, a chatter sometimes-drunkard by the name of Pennyworth who ferried her and Theodosia around for fittings and other womanly errands, had answered her constant worried looks with some bits of gossip. This was how she had learned of his habit of making the rounds to whichever venue his mother had last attended, to offer friendly overtures and seek to make amends. Keeping up appearances at all costs among his peers, while his new wife endured the madwoman in his house.

"You did not eat." A touch of disapproval in his voice.

"The pain takes my appetite. It nearly took my ability to retain my breakfast." She could not keep the resentment out of her voice. At the sound of it, he looked away again, and she did too, hands clenching around the shawl covering her, those cold, silent tears threatening again.

"I do not ask much of you—" he started, and she let out a sharp, bitter laugh that startled him.

"You ask everything of me. I must not only endure your mother's constant and unremitting complaints and insults toward everyone around, but smile and nod, and be pleasant, or she berates me for hours and threatens to beat me. I have no callers here, no one I can call friend, for no one will come to your town-house while she is here. My only company is that...that *monster* down the hall."

He sucked air in anger, and she felt his eyes on her, but she simply continued, in a low, choked voice full of more pain and despair than rage. "I can't endure this any longer." *You run away every day and leave me with her. I have no reprieve. And when you return, you expect that I shall smile for you, and be pleasant company, and play the good wife. But you...you are not a good husband!*

"I will thank you not to call my mother a monster," he said in a stiff voice. "All she requires is company—"

"What she requires is the care of a physician, for she is clearly mad!" She turned to him in anger, tears escaping from beneath her lashes. "How could you lay the burden of her upon me, your new wife? How could you force me to endure this?"

He stood suddenly, face dark. "I'm not listening to this." He turned on his heel and started walking out, back stiff.

"Coward," she spat.

He stopped dead, but he did not turn around.

She sat up fully, drawing as deep a breath as she could around her loosened corset. "You wish for me to love you, but you do not love me. Not enough to protect me from her ill use and her madness. You think that it is my duty to endure her, my husband, and pretend for everyone else, including you, that nothing is wrong. But if there was not, you would not have a problem with keeping company with her, or taking her to official functions. You *know* she antagonizes everyone she sets her sights on. You have seen the way she speaks to me. The way she speaks to everyone."

It was like a dam had broken inside of her. She knew it was improper, and so unlike her usual manner, but what had been demure gotten her? It had encouraged him to ignore her plight, and she was sick of it—and of him. "You go about every day after she has been to some party or gathering, and you spend hours making up for what she has done with our peers. But you will not consider the fact that she does damage to more than your precious reputation. She does damage to *me*. And I have grown literally sick because of it!"

She heard the rasp of his breath through his teeth as he struggled against his temper. "You will learn to endure," he said in a dull, cold voice. "We all do."

"And that is why you run away all day?"

"I am *not* running away!" he snapped, turning back to her—and then froze, the anger falling off his face, replaced by shock as he saw her expression.

"You deny my needs. You deny her cruelty. I can't stop you. I can't force you to be a good man, or a good husband, or someone with the tiniest bit of love for me." She stared hard back into his eyes, shaking inside but fueled by hot surges of rage. "But I tell you this. If you keep on cruelly burdening me with her, and treating me like a servant whom you hired to do so, one day, you will come home, and I will be gone."

He sucked air again. "Gone...?" His eyes searched hers, and he finally stammered, "Where would you go? The law binds you—"

"The law cannot bring me back from the lands of the dead. I will be free of this ill treatment, and your cowardice and neglect, even if I must hang myself to do it!" Her voice actually rose to something like a shout at the end, and he jumped a little in surprise.

There, it was said: the secret impulse that had grown in her inexorably once she had realized that her father would not help

her, and that neither her kin nor David cared one bit for her fate. The longing for oblivion that she could no longer deny. She lifted

her chin defiantly, staring back at him. *You did this to me. You and your monster of a mother.*

"But...." he started...and then he forced the shock from his face, eyes and jaw hardening. "Perhaps it is you who requires a physician, in that case!"

"Then call on one. At least then I would have someone visiting me now and again who perhaps has some semblance of a heart, and principles!" She buried her face in her hands, completely broken down by his coldness on top of everything else.

She heard him walk away slowly as she wept. The door opened, and closed; he was gone. Only then did she throw herself down on the daybed and give in to sobbing.

He did not come by any time that night to check on her. She slept more, then dully ate her cold luncheon of game hen and small potatoes, leaving the tray outside finally. She read by candlelight for a while, but the poetry kept swimming before her eyes, and finally she gave up and called in one of the servants to help her prepare for bed.

She slept, and lay awake in the dark, and slept again. Her sleep was always uneasy until she completely exhausted herself; Theodosia had a habit of pacing the halls at night, and a few alarming times Isabelle had caught the woman stealthily trying her door, which she fortunately always kept locked. Only David had the key, though after that she realized why her mother-in-law had demanded a copy, and why he kept "forgetting" to give her one. She did not know what it was that Theodosia intended to do when she sought to slip into her chambers, and that

mystery alone had turned the young wife into a very light sleeper. But this time, blessedly, nothing disturbed her, except for the

pounding of her furious, frightened heart. Eventually, though, even that could not keep her eyes from closing.

The next morning, however, she woke to an uproar: furious pounding and jiggling of the door handle, and that same hideous

bellow, more suited to an enormous, angry workman than the former wife of a Duke. "Isabelle! Isabelle! Why aren't you out of

bed? Get up! Get up, we're taking early breakfast today! Get up!" Her voice was a mad, manic yammer, as if she had drugged

herself with some awful stimulant which drove her into a frenzy. "Get up *now!*"

To Isabelle's horror, the woman started to strike and kick at the door from the other side, rattling it alarmingly in its frame.

But a moment later, she heard Maeve's voice, raised in concern. "Your Grace, please! Miss Isabelle is ill!"

"I don't care! I am *bored*, and my useless son left early!" More furious pounding. Isabelle started to shake.

"He's only stepped out to sign papers, he'll be back at the usual time for breakfast—"

"Get away from here! You are a *servant!* Stop trying to tell your better what to do!" And then the sharp sound of a slap.

Oh, poor Maeve. She heard the cook gasping—and then another slap.

"I said get away! Get back on your feet and go fix breakfast! I don't feel like waiting for my idiot son!" She went back to attacking the door. "Isabelle! *Isabelle!*"

Isabelle sobbed in terror. The sturdy English oak would not budge against that terrible woman's fists, but the shouting and violence frightened her so much that she thought her heart would jump out of her chest. *David, your heartless coward, you ran away even earlier this morning to get away from her, and this is the result! I can't believe you are my husband!*

"Get me my lantern and its oil bottle! I shall burn though this door!" came the irrational cry. "She will not escape me for much longer! She is here to entertain me! She forgets her place! Isabelle!" And more violent banging.

In desperation, Isabelle threw on her housecoat and slippers and ran to her window seat, unlatching the French panes and pushing them open. Icy wind blew against her face. She looked down wide-eyed at the courtyard a story below. Bare rosebushes, bristling with thorns, snarled up at her from below the window. No escape that way; none save the cruelest escape of all. But as the banging and tantrumming intensified outside, she started crawling out onto the ledge regardless, heart in her ears and head fogged with terror.

The family coach pulled up in the drive outside, and before it had fully come to a stop she saw David burst out of its door, coat flapping as he ran up the walk. His face was lifted toward her, and she realized he had spied her clinging to the ledge. He stumbled as his foot hit a patch of ice, but then simply grabbed one of the fence-posts beside him to steady himself and bounded on. A moment later, he disappeared inside the front door.

Mystified and quickly getting chilled, she pulled herself back in and shut the window. But that left her with her headache aggravated by Theodosia's incessant fight against the door. She was cursing now, using words Isabelle hadn't realized any woman of quality would ever consider using. But then she stopped suddenly, and she heard the woman's braying laugh.

"Oh good, you're finally back. Give me the key! I'm going to beat your recalcitrant little slut wife—"

"Get away from the door!" David yelled in a fury, and Theodosia yelped in surprise. Scrambling sounds and a thud followed, leaving Isabelle wondering what on Earth was going on.

"Why, you disrespectful little—I am your *mother*—"

"*Quiet!*" The door opened, and he bounded in, his eyes frantic. When he saw that she had pulled herself back inside, he sagged with relief.

"Isabelle!" he strode toward her, his expression half worry and half anger. "What under Heaven did you think that you were doing?"

"She was trying to break down the door," Isabelle choked out in reply, tears now icy on her cheeks and snow in her hair.

"You left again and she didn't like that I was trying to rest, and just went mad! She was threatening me! She struck Maeve twice and tried to break down the door! I was trying to find a way to escape!"

"Shut up, you filthy little—" Theodosia barreled into the room, dust on the hem of her skirt and the combs in her hair askew. Madness rode in her eyes.

David's eyes widened with fury and he turned on his mother, seizing her by the forearms and pushing her back forcibly. Theodosia let out a squawk of outrage, her eyes wide with shock as he finally stood up to her. But he was having none of it. "Take yourself out of my wife's chambers and *do not return.*"

"I am the Duchess—"

"No, you are not! Not anymore! I am Duke now, and the Duchess is in that very chamber! You are a dowager now, and we

can decide your fate! If you do not stop seeking to ruin all our lives I shall have you admitted at Bedlam like a common madwoman!"

Theodosia went white with rage and fear and screeched, striking out at him with her fists and feet. But David simply walked her back out through the door, shoved her out into the hallway, and slammed the door between them.

3: Maeve and the Clever Physician

David locked Isabelle's bedroom door, and then turned back to look at her as she perched warily on the window seat. His chest heaved as he stared at her, handsome face twisted with anguish and worry. "Are you all right?" he asked breathlessly.

She looked up at him desolately. Part of her wanted to shake her head and cry. Part of her wanted to shout at him for not doing something before now. But mostly she was pathetically grateful that he had finally done *something*, instead of just running away again.

He saw how she sat frozen, and came to her, crouching in front of her as she stayed in an awkward ball with her arms around her knees. She just stared at him, too exhausted and frightened to speak. He cupped her face and she shivered, fresh tears leaking from her eyes. Then he let out a low groan, and pulled her off the window seat and into his arms.

"I'm sorry," he murmured in her ear as he rocked her gently. "I'm so very sorry, I didn't want to believe what she was up to when I wasn't looking." It was a poor excuse; he had seen Theodosia's ranting ways for himself at many a breakfast, supper or public gathering. Granted, she got worse when she thought no one would catch her at it; she was crafty that way.

Even now, instead of pounding on the door with all her strength, she simply knocked incessantly, while calling through the door. "David? David? Open the door! I didn't mean any harm, David, just let me in, let me talk to the both of you...David?"

Isabelle shook her head as she looked up into his face. Normally, when they sat this close, she felt a flush of warmth, and sometimes dwelled on the nights they had spent together. But now, the circle of his arms was cold comfort, and she shivered against him. "You should have listened. She threatens me, she beats the servants, she tries to get into my room at night. *When are you going to do something about her?*"

David hesitated. "I... will instruct her to leave you alone from now on," he ventured, and she almost screamed with exasperation.

"That won't stop her! She does as she pleases when you are not around, and often when you are!" The knocking and terribly-reasonable chattering had not let up, even for a second. "Can you not hear how she is, even now? This is how she is when she keeps her madness *at bay*. When you are not around--"

David frowned at her, his expression closing again, though he didn't let her go. "I must deal with one issue at a time or nothing will end up properly handled. For now, I have summoned a physician to see about your headaches."

She stared at him, and then heaved a gentle sigh. Too much to expect that he would find the fullness of his courage in a single effort. Too much to expect that he might finally be taking safeguarding her seriously. But at least it was *something*. "Very well. Please send him up when he arrives."

"Will you not be joining us for meals?" His baffled disappointment made her headache return.

"My husband, I would rather throw myself out that window than deal with your mother again today. I have exceeded my limit with dealing with her, and if you cannot or will not recognize that, then I do not wish to keep company with you either."

His mouth worked, but he finally nodded. "I'll...have Maeve come up with your breakfast, then," he murmured, tone disappointed. "The physician said he would be here before luncheon."

"Very well, I will be ready for him." Her voice came out a sigh.

His grip tightened on her, and he kissed the top of her head, whether in tenderness or apology, she could not tell. But then he picked her up, and gently carried her to her day-bed. "I'll send up one of the servants to help you dress."

When he left, a cheerfully yammering Theodosia tried to shove herself into the room again, her smile a leer and her eyes fixed hungrily past him, on Isabelle. He immediately took her by the forearms again and walked her back out of the room while she whined in protest. The door slammed behind them, and Isabelle hurried up to make sure it was locked before settling back down on the day bed.

"So... your husband said that you have had nervous difficulty and headaches," Dr. Martins said softly as he sat across from her in one of her sitting-room chairs. Dressed, cleaned up and properly coiffed, Isabelle perched again on the window seat, watching the red-haired, lanky physician a little warily.

"I do not wish to make my husband appear inattentive," she replied quietly. "But such is the case here. I do not suffer because of my nervous problems. I suffer because of the Dowager Duchess's nervous problems."

"Ah, Theodosia," he said with a knowing look of irritation. She blinked at him in surprise, wondering just how infamous her irrational, contentious mother-in-law had become in London. "She has refused all treatment for her moral insanity, and used her position to reinforce it. Otherwise, I suspect that she would be undergoing full-time treatment at one of the small asylums set aside for the gentry. There are several in Kent."

"Moral insanity?" Isabelle looked at him in honest confusion. She had never heard the term before.

"Yes. Moral insanity coupled with mania, as best as we who were consulted on her case can determine. Her husband struggled for years to find her a diagnosis that would lead to proper treatment. But he refused to sign her over to an asylum, or permit the use of the water cure or similar modes of treatment. He called them cruel." He held out his hand for hers and she offered it; he took her pulse, frowning thoughtfully.

"What *is* moral insanity?"

"It is a disorder of the moral and social sense," he replied. "Intellect, cognition, and the capacity for rational thought are largely unimpaired. Yet the sufferer lacks, for want of a better word, any form of moral restraint which might prevent her from acting on any negative impulse that enters her head. Her excessive pride prevents her from being able to perceive the harm she does to others, and her instability is always excused away by her delusions about herself and the world. She is *capable* of behaving properly, and considering others, but cannot be convinced of the rightness of any action that is inconvenient to her ambitions."

"Then she is wicked, as well as mad."

He smiled ruefully, the crows' feet deepening at the corners of his bright blue eyes. "In a sense, that is quite correct. She is not entirely responsible for her actions, but her moral sense has been badly stunted, and unlike the motives of the truly mad, she takes no small amount of pleasure in her outrageous behavior. It does not help that she was excessively spoiled by her parents, and deferred to in many things by her husband."

She sighed. "I do not know why His Grace has chosen to assign you to me instead of her. She is the source of any disturbance that I may be experiencing."

He frowned and nodded. "I had thought as much when he described your troubles. Though he spoke of you threatening to kill yourself...?"

She sighed, looking out the window. The snow was thawing, patches of brown and green showing through where it had formerly blanketed the front lawn. "He insisted on my 'getting used to' playing nursemaid for that...creature out there. His idea of wifely duties seems entirely centered on having someone to shield him from as much contact with his mother as possible. I warned him that I would leave if he continued, even if my only recourse was suicide. It is not that I wish to destroy myself. It is that I will not allow *her* to continue to destroy me."

The doctor sat back in his seat, eyebrows going up. "Given the extremes of the experiences that you described to me, it seems clear that you are no more mentally disturbed than I. Your melancholy stems entirely from her influence; were her behavior corrected, you would no longer experience it."

"Is it...possible for you to explain this to my husband?" she asked softly. "I had to crawl out on the window-ledge to try and escape his mother before he would take what I have been saying seriously."

The doctor offered her a thin smile. "I am sorry, but you see, the only people who can "get used to" a woman such as his mother are those who grew up around such behavior. He did not view what you have experienced as particularly troubling until he saw for himself that it damages you, because he was expected to put up with the same for years without complaint."

"Yet he avoids her as much as he can himself."

"Yes, well." His smile went a little sad. "The mind is a tricky thing, and even as we tell ourselves one thing, our impulse may well express the secrets of our heart. And sometimes a man's pride may halt his admission of any vulnerability at all." He brought his great, square black physician's case out from behind his chair, and opened the snaps. "At any rate, I believe I have some solutions to some of these issues available."

She blinked at him in surprise, as he had agreed with her assessment that she herself was not ill—but as always when presented an opportunity to learn, she peered into the case curiously. Little bottles, tins and jars, each in their own loop and each labeled in a neat hand: aromatic vinegars, herbal powders, preparations of laudanum and cannabis, and an assortment of small, sharp knives, needles, linen strips and coils of cat gut. "What is all of this?"

"Oh, they're for an assortment of ailments, depending. It is best to bring the whole case when I call on a patient in their home, for oftentimes more is going on with their health than the ailment which made the m call upon me."

"I see. And in this case?"

He held up a small bottle of dark yellow-green fluid. "This is an aromatic vinegar which should help with your headaches. Do you have a vinaigrette?"

She nodded, and went to retrieve it from her dressing room: a small box of gold filigree, suspended on a chain and containing a sponge cut to fit its interior exactly. He took this, and added some of the sharp-smelling fluid to it. "Use this regularly upon the first onset of symptoms. You should find relief in a few minutes."

She sniffed. The vinegar smell grew less potent as the concoction was exposed to air, and slowly the florals underneath asserted themselves strongly. "Is that lavender?"

"Among a few others, but yes, primarily." He had a strange, fey little smile on, and she wondered at it. But before she could ask, he bent again over the case, and retrieved a much larger

bottle, wide-mouthed, and full of a thick-looking liquid. "Now, this, I can only give to you if you assure me that you have no

impulse to self-destruction that cannot be cured by an alleviation of your circumstances."

She looked at the bottle, and then back at him. "I swear it is so, Doctor."

"Very well, then. This is a sedative preparation of my own devising, which in sufficient quantity can calm the most agitated nerves and induce sleep. A thimbleful is more than sufficient;

twice that will leave a subject sleepy and exceedingly relaxed. Beyond that is dangerous."

She nodded, staring at it, wondering if there was laudanum in it. That would explain the danger, at least. "How shall I use it?"

"It can be introduced in strong drinks and food, and be undetectable by the consumer. It is a little bitter otherwise, so I suggest this method." Again, that faint gleam of mischief in his eye. "I will see that your husband knows these instructions as well, in case you get confused."

It was a bit condescending, but he was a doctor and she a young woman, and she thought for a moment on the irony of his mention of being expected to put up with things without complaint. She could sympathize a bit more with her husband once she made the connection, and nodded. "I shall remember. Does it act quickly?"

"Within half an hour. The alcohol it is dissolved in aids in its speedy distribution within the body." He looked at her curiously. "You are quite a bit more curious about matters medical than most ladies of quality to whom I attend. Was your father a physician?"

"No, I merely read a great deal." She offered him a polite smile as she rose. "Thank you, Doctor. When will you return?"

"I will return within one week to see how things progress. If there is trouble, send a messenger." He stood and snapped his case closed, then scooped it up under one arm. "I shall visit with your husband and then see myself out. Good day, Your Grace."

Once he was gone, she uncorked the bottle and sniffed the faint bitterness of the contents, and frowned. She did not feel safe taking a strong sedative when Theodosia was still in the habit of creeping around at night. But perhaps it could calm her fears next time that madwoman pounded fruitlessly at her door. She set it aside in a drawer for now. But meanwhile, she looped the vinaigrette's chain around her neck. It was almost time for luncheon.

Theodosia yammered on all lunch, complaining about how bored and unattended-to she had been all morning thanks to Isabelle's illness, about her poor treatment by her ungrateful son, and about how that red-haired doctor had stared at her on her way out the door. On and on and on, as meanwhile Isabelle nibbled on the contents of her plate without much looking at or tasting it. Her headache started to bloom; she took the cover off her vinaigrette and took a deep sniff of the contents.

"Ugh!" Theodosia dropped her fork suddenly. "What is that horrific scent?"

"It is my vinaigrette, Your Grace. The doctor has placed me on a preparation of aromatics for my headaches." She kept her voice even and kind, but Theodosia grew more agitated with every second. "I am required to keep it with me for attacks."

"That doctor! Oh, no wonder, he hates me so! He knows how much I despise lavender! Ugh!" She stood up and made her usual shooing-off gesture. "Go eat in your chambers, you're stinking up the entire dining room."

Isabelle took her plate and fled gratefully, wondering. *An aromatic vinegar for your headaches.* Headaches which the doctor knew were caused by enduring Theodosia's presence. *Did he know? Did he choose lavender on purpose?*

Slowly, slowly, understanding dawned on her. And she smiled. Going to her drawer, she took out the bottle of strong sedative. *To be mixed in food or drink.* Suddenly she realized as well why he had given her this particular sedative, and her smile widened and grew a little fey. She wrapped the bottle in her shawl's edge, and hurried out, heading down to the kitchens.

"I need your help," she said to Maeve as soon as she had drawn the cook into the larder for privacy.

Maeve just smiled. "Oh do you, then?" Her expression was so knowing that it startled Isabelle.

"I do. The Doctor was just here, and he gave me this sedative. It's to be introduced in food or drink--"

"Oh, I already know, child, he told me before he left. Have you not noticed the similarities in our coloring? Doctor Shea is in fact my cousin. I told him of your predicament at once I discovered it."

Isabelle's eyes widened. "You...you both planned this?"

"I told you you had more friends here than you might think." She winked, and patted Isabelle on the arm as the young wife sobbed quietly with relief. "Now, let's see what we can do with this." She took the bottle and peered at it. "Two tea-spoons of this stuff should do the trick!"

At supper that evening, Theodosia sat, unusually quiet as she slowly ate her meal. A deep calm seemed to have settled over her, quieting her agitation and rage. David watched her the entire time, a baffled expression on his face that was so comedic Isabelle had to fight a bout of giggling as she watched him in turn.

The Dowager Duchess dozed off eventually, snoring lightly until two of the maidservants came to lead her off to bed.

"You did something, didn't you? You're smiling too much to have not done something." Her husband had followed her to her chambers after supper, and watched as she took off her vinaigrette filled with harridan-repellent and set it carefully aside on her dressing-table.

"It is our physician's doing, not mine. I merely explained the nature of my affliction, and he took steps to treat it."

"By *drugging* my mother's food?" He sounded like he was struggling to disapprove, and she just smiled wider.

"Well, Husband," she said softly as she took the combs from her hair and let her curls spill over her shoulders, "It is a far better solution than letting her constant agitation and bitterness sour every day, for herself as well as us."

He stared at her in amazement. "Why, you...clever, naughty little minx! To think you would conspire with our own physician-
-"

"To solve an affliction that has made the whole family suffer, driven off servants and damaged your family's reputation? Not to mention, nearly made me flee?"

He blinked several times, sounding slightly indignant. "Well, I never said that you're being a naughty little minx was a bad thing." He came over to her, nudging against her with his eyelids lowered, hands sliding up her arms.

Her smile widened. "Oh, good!" She tilted her head back and he kissed her, mouth suddenly hungry on hers and a look of deep relief on his face.

It was underhanded, and terrible. But more terrible still would have been to do nothing. And apparently her husband's relief at the reprieve was so great that it broke the pane of ice that had risen between them thanks to Theodosia's madness. She returned his kiss as his busy fingers broke the stitches on her bodice and tugged her dress down.

In the uncommon quiet of the house, with the door locked and no one rattling at the knob on the other side, they undressed each other, and settled into the draped, quilt-piled bed she had occupied alone for days. He was learning her slowly since their wedding night, and covered her with kisses, fingers sliding over her breasts and hips and back, teasing at her until he heard her breath catch and come out in whimpers.

Only then, once she clung to him and her hips moved of themselves under his hands, did he settle himself over her and press his manhood into her waiting body. She moaned into his mouth as he surged against her, his big, lanky body shivering with each movement until he was panting for air. The minutes swam as they both grew frantic, hearts pounding against each other.

Finally, her head fell back, and she sobbed with release; he moved more fiercely, galloping against her and making the bed creak under them. He joined her soon in ecstasy, pushing down on her with low shouts until he shuddered a last time and went limp over her.

They lay together after, and as she saw him staring at the underside of the canopy, she spoke softly. "I understand that this solution is imperfect, my husband. But so is the situation."

"True." He smiled lazily and rolled over to bury his nose in her hair. "I look forward at least to having more time to spend at home with you."

"Good," she murmured as she drifted off. They slept deeply, sweetly together, and for once, the house was quiet enough in the morning to let them linger.

******

THE END

Enjoy what you read? Please keep flipping to the end of the book to leave a review on Amazon. Thanks!

Winning the Duke's Heart

Historical Regency Romance

*****

1: The Newlywed and the Mysterious Book

What am I doing? Emily gripped the edge of the coach window as they jolted along the cobblestone streets through London, the panicked question echoing in her head. *Why on Earth did I ever agree to this?*

Emily, youngest daughter of the Earl of Harcourt, had never been to London before. She had spent her whole life on her father's estate in Oxford—most of it sharpening her nose in his extensive library. Emily had never met a book she did not like, and because she was well read, she had always fancied herself as an experienced sophisticate. But now, at eighteen, and in the midst of being packed off to marry a total stranger in London, she was starting to realize just how naive she really was.

"What is that terrible smell?" she asked softly, her wide blue eyes watering slightly as it choked her nostrils. She was the product of a sickly youth and a little delicate still, her skin a shade too pale as she tried to peer out through the curtains. She caught sight of a narrow lane crowded in by buildings and clogged with coaches, most far plainer than her father's. But she saw it all through a yellowish film that clung to the window, running down into brown droplets at the bottom of the glass.

"That's London on a summer morning, dear." Her single maidservant, a chubby, ruddy-faced Irishwoman named Annie who had practically raised her, clucked her tongue. "Don't be showing your face out the coach windows, it's not proper while we're riding through town."

"Ugh, Annie. Everything in the world's 'not proper'. I at least should be allowed to see where I'm going." She puffed a curl out of her eyes grumpily, but let the green velvet curtain fall back into place. Her handmaid just smiled a little and shook her head, too polite to roll her eyes.

"Oh, don't fuss, dear. This isn't the Oxford estate. London's upper crust is full of gossips, and they will pick you to pieces if you give them an inch. Be on your best behavior, at least in public, and you'll thank yourself later."

Annie and she were opposites physically. Annie was big and bluff, her round belly belying her strength and her red face illustrating health so robust that she had survived a plague in her youth. She dressed plainly in gray uniform and white apron, her dark, wavy hair pinned up and covered by a crisp kerchief. Emily was small and slightly fragile-looking, her eyes almost overlarge, her pale gold curls tumbling rebelliously from her chignon and her cream-colored gown and shawl lending to her air of delicacy. She wore little in the way of jewelry, just a single strand of pearls and earrings to match the new wedding ring that sat unfamiliarly on her finger. Unlike the cheap silver claddagh on Annie's thick finger, it was a richly-wrought, delicately-colored thing, with a circle of pearls surrounding a single, faceted pink spinel. It had apparently belonged to the Duke's grandmother, and it was the only thing about her new life arrangement that Emily liked at all.

Thomas, Duke of Wellington, recently ascended after the death of his father, was the coldest man she had ever met in her life. At their wedding, held with just their families and a few witnesses at a vicarage just outside Oxford, he had barely touched her enough to slip the ring on and place a light kiss on her cheek. Bitter disappointment for Emily, whom he had then sent away to pack her things, without spending any more time with her than he absolutely had to. Having grown up on the romances in her late mother's collection, and her father's loving reminiscences of his darling wife, she had thought that marriage and love simply went together, neat as a story in one of her books.

One look into the Duke's frosty gray eyes had disabused her of that notion entirely. And perhaps she should have known, she thought sadly as she fiddled with the ring. It was an arranged marriage, mostly used to solidify business and land deals between Harcourt and Wellington. Her father had been delighted to have her "marrying up"; the Duke was wealthy as well as powerful, and enjoyed regular correspondences with the Crown. And as for Emily, she had heartily agreed at the time— while staring at a portrait of the man she would come to marry.

She had spent two months daydreaming over that portrait, staring up at that long, pale face, those broad shoulders, the way his strapping build filled out his naval uniform. She had fancied that those silvery eyes hid a kind soul, and tried to imagine what color his hair was under his rather plain powdered wig. As it turned out, his hair was dark brown and wavy, and he kept it cropped short; the wig was for the Palace, and for portraiture. That had only charmed her more; on laying eyes on him in the flesh for the first time she had caught herself wondering what those short, dark curls would feel like under her fingers.

And then he had looked right through her, and spent their introduction in her father's parlor speaking to her as little as possible. She had noticed at the time that he appeared to be a man of few words in general, an impression that had not improved even once she had gone from being Lady Emily Harcourt to the Duchess Wellington. It was as if he considered most people around him to not be worth talking to. And what broke her heart was that she could not bring herself to disdain him in return. She couldn't forget those sweet days of gazing on his portrait, and her infatuation lingered even as his indifference bruised her heart.

"You're broody as a hen today," Annie said gently, reaching over to touch her slim hand with two fingers. "It's not so terrible, Emmy dear." Only together could they be so informal; a hug here and there and Annie's use of pet names, as if she were a younger sister, had done much to comfort Emily through the aching years without a mother, and she didn't resent it now. "He's not so bad, this Duke."

"I think he's a monster," Emily pouted sadly in response, her eyes still seeking out the bits of view she could spy between the window and the curtain. "I've never met anyone so heartless. He barely looks at me."

Annie just gave her a sad smile. "Oh, my poor dear. Bless your heart, you're so innocent sometimes." She drew a breath and hesitated, then shook her head, firming her round jaw a little. "There are many husbands who are worse than cold, dear. There are those who drink, and lie, and cheat, and will keep you in line with their fists. There are worse, even. The Duke's no monster. He's simply walking about in a sort of armor, here, inside." She tapped her ample bosom. "I spied him out when he visited. He's not cruel. He's protecting himself from something. That one has a secret, Emmy, and once you find it, you'll have your proper chance at winning his heart."

"How can you be so certain, Annie?" She looked back at her maid in astonishment. The middle-aged Irishwoman was always wise, but this seemed almost prescient.

"Ah, it's no trick." Annie smiled, the corners of her eyes crinkling slightly. "I raised five brothers for my Dad after Mum died, and who do you think they go to with their women troubles to this day? I've too much experience knowing the hearts of young men."

"Wouldn't things be a bit different for my husband, though?" She didn't want to be rude, but their stations and life circumstances had to have an effect.

"Bah, farmer, porter, soldier, Duke, a young man's heart is a young man's heart. And your young man is guarding his. See what you can do to win his trust, and that will change." Her maid winked, and then went back to her knitting, somehow able to keep her hands steady despite the jolting carriage.

Soon after, they were forced to a stop in the middle of an intersection. A carter had overloaded his wagon, and the whole mess had tipped back onto the street. It stuck up at an angle, spilling canvas-wrapped bundles into the road and leaving a confused-looking donkey dangling from its harness in front. The carter and his assistant were busy pulling enough bundles off the cart to get the donkey's hooves back to solid ground, all the while yelling and swearing at each other in an unintelligible accent.

Emily peeked out at the scene curiously, Annie's admonition forgotten as she watched the scene unfold. A gorgeous French-made carriage with four matched gray geldings stopped nearby; a very elegantly-dressed man poked his bewigged head out and shook his fist, shouting at the carter in French. Emma didn't understand a word, but his tone was absolutely unmistakable. She was stifling a nervous giggle when she saw something happened that horrified her.

As the Frenchman slammed his coach door, a slim, plainly-bound book slid off of his lap and fell through the gap before it closed. It bounced off the footrest, and then fell to the cobbles, inches from a mud puddle. Emily gasped and opened the door of her coach, leaning out to cry a warning to the Frenchman's driver. But a gap in the coach traffic had opened before the elegant carriage, and before she could do more than draw breath, it sped away again. "Oh no!"

"Come back in, Emmy, what are you doing making a scene?" Annie's voice was sharp, and Emily pulled her head back in and shut the door.

"He dropped his book! It will be ruined if I don't rescue it!" She couldn't stand the idea of it. Her father had always impressed on her the value of books, even cheaply made ones. Books, he always said, were the keys to learning and imagination, and both were very important to living well.

Annie did roll her eyes this time, but her smile was kind. She knew Emily's feelings on the matter. "Fine, fine, stay here, I'll go after it myself. Looks like we'll be here for a bit anyway." Heaving herself off the seat, the big woman opened the coach door and stepped out, looking around briefly. None of the coaches in the middle section of the jam-up could move until the carter got his burdens off the road, so she was able to simply walk right across the intersection, scoop up the book, and come back with it, humming a little to herself as she did so.

"There we go," she said, holding out the book as she clambered back inside. She shut the door and settled into her seat as Emily took the book gingerly and examined it.

It had a few droplets of mud on it, which she wiped away with the inside of her handkerchief, folding the clean cloth at the edges over the soiled before tucking it back in her reticule. She turned it over, looking at the plain stamped cover with a little frown. "It's in French, of course. Now I wish I'd studied it a little while I was learning my Latin." She pouted gently as she peered at the title. "The only word I can make out is 'Philosophy'. And the author is a Marquis."

"Philosophy's a respectable enough subject for a book. Wonder why it's printed up cheap, like a romance serial?" Annie squinted at it curiously.

"It's obviously a student copy. Or...something like that. At any rate, I suppose there's no chance we'll see him again. But I'd like to at least keep the book from being ruined."

"Well, I doubt there will be any surprise that you show up with a volume of something or other under your arm, dear. Your reputation precedes you, and that's not a terrible thing in this case. There's no scandal in being bookish. Perhaps the Duke's library has a philosophy section."

"Yes, perhaps it would make an endearing gift." *It would be lovely if I could find something to endear me to him.* She riffled through the pages, which had no engravings and were closely typeset in equally impenetrable French. "I suppose he'll know French. I'll have to ask him."

She looked at the cover again. *La Philosophie Dans Le Boudoir.* Wasn't "boudoir" another word for a bedroom? Now she really wished that she had studied the language. "What an odd title," she murmured. "Ah well." She tucked it under her arm, and draped her shawl over it for safekeeping as she settled in for a long wait. Hopefully their late arrival would not trouble the Duke too much.

*****

2: The Duke and the Marquis

It took an extra hour for them to get to the Duke's townhouse near the Palace. It was a strange, aging mansion of dark wood, gray stone and white plasters, its windows small and deep-set. It sat in the midst of a gated garden that was mostly rolling lawn at the back, with a formal garden spreading along the entry path to greet visitors. Their driver took them to the entrance and then went on to the coach-house; he would bring their bags up later. Emily sighed relief as she alighted from the coach and could finally stretch her legs a little. The scent of the garden in the rain pushed the stench of the city streets from her nostrils, and she peered around at the hedges and flowers with a tiny smile. *Perhaps my new home won't be so bad.*

It was too overcast to need a parasol. Annie trailed after her with it tucked under her arm instead, while Emily took her little walk up to the broad front steps.

As she drew near the base of the steps, the door banged open and the Duke strode out, hair loose, without a coat, his eyes a little wild. His manservant Portman trailed after him, tailcoat flapping behind him, his round, lined face a little red from exertion and surprise. "Your Grace, your coat and cane!" he called after—and then saw Emily there, blinking up at them. "...Oh dear," Portman said ruefully, his watery hazel eyes full of pained embarrassment.

Emily stood in shock as the Duke hurried down the stairs toward her. He had a strange look on his face: an almost blank look of panic slowly melting into relief. *What is this? He couldn't care less about me.*

To her absolute amazement, he took her by the shoulders, just a little roughly in his panic, his ungloved hands shockingly warm through the silk. He looked her in the face searchingly— and then finally, he spoke. Every word seemed forced out, as if he had to focus very hard on speaking. "A-are...are y-you well, my Lady?"

The broken syllables confused her for a moment, as much as the sudden contact—and his obvious worry. "Yes, my Lord, I am. There was an accident in the street on the way, and we were held there while it was cleared." The worry in his eyes made her heart jump into her throat, and she said hastily, "I am so very sorry if I caused trouble by being late."

He paused, blinking at her, and then said in a lower, cooler voice, "No, of course. A travel issue. I s-sh...." He stopped and squinted in frustration. "I should h-have known." He smiled tightly and stepped back, gesturing toward the entrance with a little bow.

His manservant stood awkwardly at the top of the stairs and watched them climb them together, his expression a strange mixture of scandalized, awkward and pleased. He held the door for them as they came through, and Annie trailed after them, taking Emma's shawl for her as they stopped in the sweeping entryway. It was glassed in, giving it a greenhouse look accentuated by the vines clambering the pains from without. A white staircase swooped down from the second floor, gleaming in contrast against the dark wood floor with its Oriental rugs.

Emily was so busy looking around at it all that her grip on the book loosened, and when Annie tugged off her shawl it knocked the volume to the floor with a thump. "Oh!" she said in soft shock, and started to duck down for it out of habit—only to find the Duke crouching at her feet.

He gazed up at her, his clear gray eyes twinkling briefly with amusement as he retrieved the book from the floor for her. He straightened, and offered it to her, the tiniest smile on his lips. Again, a complete change. It was as if he had a charming but equally quiet twin who had been hiding in the townhouse, and now pretended to be his brother.

But then his eyes chanced to settle on the book's cover, and read was was written there. She supposed that he did read French, for his expression shifted immediately. First puzzled...and then slowly....

His eyes went very wide, and flicked from her to the book and back again. He blinked so many times that she wondered if he had gotten something in his eye. And then, going pale, he turned and hurried off suddenly. He took the stairs two at a time, the book still clenched forgotten in his hand, and quickly vanished from sight into the east wing.

Emily looked from the stairs, to Portman, to Annie, and shook her head in astonishment. "What in the world was that all about?"

"I'm certain I don't know, your Grace," sighed Portman, who seemed used to the Duke's eccentricities. "Your husband has his own way of doing things." His narrowed eyes and tentative tone showed his gingerness in approaching the subject, and she just sighed and nodded quietly.

"I understand. Or I will try to. Please let me know if my Lord should call for me. We will be putting my chambers in order." She had to fight down a tremor in her voice, but managed to sound at least a little confident.

He bowed, and led them up the stairs and into the west wing, which was lined with tall doors facing a wall of equally tall, narrow windows. They overlooked the garden, and she paused to look down on it from above, smiling a little again. She spied a little bench under an apple tree which looked just perfect for reading in good weather. If she could sort out life with the Duke's eccentricities, it would be a lovely spot for her to claim as her own.

Portman opened the suite at the far end for them and handed her the key. "Your Grace, if you need anything, please send down your maidservant." It was a polite but totally unnecessary reminder, and she looked at him in mild surprise. She wondered if it was custom for members of this family to sequester themselves. It certainly appeared to be the Duke's practice. "We will call you for supper."

"Of course." She dismissed him, and then turned worriedly to Annie once the door closed behind him. "What did I do?" she whispered in a near panic. "He was actually being rather nice for a moment there, and then he went and ran off with my book!"

"Don't quite understand it myself, dear," she admitted kindly. "He seemed rather shocked by whatever that book is you picked up in the square. I suppose he speaks French. Perhaps he's got no love for the subject of philosophy?"

"I don't know. It's all quite strange, Annie. He's quite strange."

"Not so strange. I can see straightaway now why he doesn't talk so much." Annie's eyes twinkled a little. There was a knock at the door, and the porter came in with their bags, setting them inside before retreating with a bow. She held the door for him, and closed it firmly behind him before continuing. "Emmy, dear, the man has a stutter! That's why he has no love of long conversations—especially not with a new wife he's trying to impress!"

"A stutter?" she thought back. His words, his inflections, the deep concentration and flashes of frustration on his face as he spoke. "Does it get worse when he's nervous, then?"

"Always," Annie said ruefully. "Poor thing. If knowledge of it became widespread he'd get snickered at behind his back all the time amongst his peers. Terrible, really, but that is how it goes."

"That's why he doesn't speak. Especially in public. He doesn't want anyone to notice." Astonishment, relief and sympathy washed over her, and she quickly settled into a chair near the door. "I thought he disliked me!"

"Oh no, were that the case I suspect he wouldn't have worried when you were late." Annie's eyes twinkled, and Emily heaved as big a sigh as her corset would allow. At least now she understood a little bit about her mysterious new husband. Though why he had looked so shocked, and then run off with her new book, she still didn't understand.

The Duke's strange behavior continued that evening, when she was called to dinner, and sat in silence at the far end of a long table from him. She ate her roast duck and vegetables, watching his face as he silently devoured his portion and refused to do more than glance her way. His face was pale, his expression preoccupied; he even seemed a little nervous. When she caught him looking at her, a flicker almost of panic seemed to enter his gray eyes, and he looked away quickly, a flash of anger and frustration replacing it. His expressive face stayed a mystery. She longed to confront him, but he seemed so easily shocked and upset by the strangest things, and she wondered if her boldness would be even more off-putting for him. Feeling frozen, she ate mechanically, hoping he would eventually bring up whatever was troubling him.

Instead, the entire meal passed just that way: silent, so disappointingly so that she didn't quite know what to do with herself. After he finished eating, he excused himself, and retired to his rooms. She looked down at her half-eaten meal, and felt tears well up behind her eyes, making her head hurt. *What is it now?*

Three days passed in that exact same way, as her apprehensions and sadness grew, curdling in the pit of her stomach, poisoning whatever optimism she had been trying to cultivate about her new home and marriage. They only saw each other during meals, and when they did he simply did not speak to her at all. All he offered were those nervous glances, sometimes edged with longing, sometimes edged with ice.

She tried to stave off her loneliness with walks in the garden, Annie trailing after her with shawl and parasol handy. In the garden's relative privacy they could talk a little, and Emily could confide a little about her feelings. Otherwise, there were her chambers—but after too many hours shut up in them she always started to feel like a prisoner. So the garden it was: walking slowly along muddy paths, trying to keep her voice low.

"I'm positive that he hates me now," she said in pure exasperation on the third day. The two of them were sitting on the bench under the apple tree, watching a flock of sparrows pour into and out of the hedges in twittering streams. "I've no idea at all what I did, Annie. And I have no idea why he took my book, or what he's done with it!"

"Well, he's *your* husband. It may not be proper strictly speaking, but he's not about to go sniffing about propriety too much with the way he acts when he's on his own property. Did you see him running about like a boy the first day we got here?" Annie patted her shoulder gently. "If you're troubled by it, or think his shyness about that stutter might get in the way, write him a note. It's a bit silly, but it has precedent."

"So I should write him a love note, then?" She blushed slightly, thinking about it. *Should I tell him about the portrait?*

Annie's eyes twinkled. "Well, I didn't say anything about it being a *love* note, but...." she looked at Emily, and just smiled. "Yes. Perhaps a love note is just the thing. I'll fetch you some stationery and a pen and ink."

*****

3: Words of Love and Lust

Emily labored for most of an evening on the letter. She was a good writer, but had no idea how to write of love to a man. She had exchanged correspondences with many female friends in her younger days, scribbling passages that breathlessly described whatever her latest desperate crush was in the sort of detail only giggly teenage girls would obsess over. She wrote letters to her father every few days, reassuring him that things were well when they honestly weren't. But the sort of feelings that were going into this letter, she had never expected to share with anyone.

My Lord,

Since my arrival, we have barely spoken. I understand that you are a man of few words, but as it stands I feel that I, your wife, remain a stranger to you. As little as I know of love, its profession or its actions, still I wonder how I have offended you so that you would ignore me so completely.

If it is because we were set at each other by our parents, and had no say, please consider that you are not alone in this. I too am in this position, and I too am still finding my footing on the path our families have laid before us. If anyone can sympathize with your discomfort, I can, if you will allow it.

If it is something about me which you have come to dislike, I would prefer that you would tell me, so I might correct it. We have known each other but days, and then barely. Given a chance I am certain I can overcome any trouble or misunderstanding that has arisen.

If it is something about you that you think I would dislike, then I beg you give me a chance again to prove that it is no barrier between us. I am neither haughty nor cruel, and I owe you my faithfulness and patience as your wife.

I beg that you will consider speaking with me honestly on whatever matter troubles you, that we may lay it to rest and continue on together.

With all sincerity,

Emily Wellington

She felt a little sick with nervousness as she crept down the hall toward her husband's suite. He always worked behind closed doors, scribbling away at something or quietly reading. She stood nervously outside of his door, feeling childish and stupid, and wishing she dared simply confront him. But Annie had reminded her over and over that discretion was important in London. Raised voices gave the opportunity to overhear things, and in doing so, create gossip. The last thing she wanted was to invite scandal into his door. If she did so he would end up disliking her even more.

Finally, hands and lips both trembling with apprehension, and worry and despair nipping at her heart, Emily slipped the note under the door. She couldn't bring herself to stay long enough to hear if he walked over and took it. Instead she turned and hurried off, back to her room. She closed the door and threw herself on her bed, heart pounding. *Please let something good come of this.*

She didn't see the Duke at breakfast. Her heart sank as she stared across the table at his empty chair. She tried to force down some bites of toast and eggs and treacle, but everything turned sideways in her mouth, which felt dry as the top of a gravestone.

The letter didn't work. Now he doesn't even want to look at me. Alone in the echoing dining hall, she felt the tears start to run down her cheeks. Finally unable to control it any longer, she put her head down on her arms and sobbed.

She didn't hear anyone come in while she was crying. She kept on, shameless, tear-staining her sleeves like a child and not caring at all. It felt like she was being bled of some poison that was threatening her heart. She didn't know how much time had passed, but when she finally lifted her head again, Portman was sitting at the table a few chairs away.

Oh no. Now I've made a fool of myself. She blinked back at him in astonishment, her cheeks heating up so badly she expected the tears to rise off them like steam.

In return he offered a sad little smile, and an inclination of his head. "I beg Your Grace's pardon for this intrusion, but I fear the circumstances are a bit exceptional."

"What do you mean?"

"I was sent to give you a letter in response to the one you so recently wrote. You were correct in assuming that His Grace prefers correspondence to conversation much of the time. But circumstances being what they are, I believe its delivery to be less important than the current issue."

She dabbed at her eyes with her table napkin ungracefully, her handkerchief already sodden. Without a word, he pulled his own from his pocket and offered it; she nodded thanks and switched to using it. "And...what issue is that?" she asked finally.

"Pardon my impertinence, Your Grace. But the one who should be asking this seems rather preoccupied with that book you arrived with, so it seems that the duty falls to me." A layer of his formality slipped away, and concern filled his eyes. "And thus I must dare to ask...are you quite well?"

She stared at him, shocked not by his concern, but rather that he had dared be so informal when she was still largely an unknown in this household. He did not know if she was a gossip or not, or how strictly she adhered to formality. But the shock simply pushed more tears from her eyes, and she swallowed and had to wipe her face again. "No, Portman, I am not. Thank you for asking."

"I see." He drew a deep breath. "It is not my place to be critical of His Grace or his behavior. But a man needs no title to have a sense of chivalry, and I daresay I cannot stand by untroubled by Your Grace's tears when I have a daughter your very age at home."

She gave him a sad, grateful smile. "Your consideration is appreciated, Portman. But I can't imagine you know the answer to this mystery, if my husband is not in the habit of talking to people."

"Oh, he'll talk to me." His smile gentled at her surprise. "Behind closed doors, when in a calm environment, he speaks with me quite regularly." He leaned forward a little. "Have you guessed why he speaks so little in public?"

"It's a stutter, is it not?"

"Indeed. And one he is careful to conceal. For weeks before the wedding he expressed his concern over what you would say once this was discovered."

"That is so ironic. He need never have worried. I...I don't *care* that he stutters. I do a bit when I'm nervous as well. But I suppose he'd assume I would do as others would. I imagine he has gotten ill treatment for his trouble."

"Oh yes." He nodded gently, his expression tired. "Especially from the old Duke. And so His Grace is a recluse, and nearly mute in public, and with anyone he does not know well." He spoke low, his tone comforting and a little conspiratorial. "His correspondences are among the most sought-after in London, as he is quite articulate...in print. But the risk when he opens his mouth...."

"I'll keep his secret to my grave if it comes to it. It is as I said. I wish for him to feel free to speak with me." She wiped her face again. "As it is, he avoids me altogether. It is as if he hates me."

"He does not hate you, Your Grace," he replied gently. "When your coach was delayed, he was beside himself. He told me that he feared you had changed your mind, because he had been unable to speak much at all at your wedding."

She stared at him, astounded. *The Duke fears I would see him as a cripple. Him! The man I dreamed of for months before I even saw him.* "No, I merely...worried I had done something wrong without realizing. London manners are so sensitive, not like those of the country estates." Or rather, her father's estate.

"He does not dislike you, Your Grace. Though I admit that his strange obsession with that book, and his complete avoidance of you, those are unusual." He winced thoughtfully. "I haven't any advice on that, aside of asking that you understand that His Grace is a very passionate and eccentric man. For example, for reasons I do not understand, he insisted on writing his correspondence to you in French." He removed a folded, sealed letter from inside the wing of his jacket, and passed it to her.

She took it and opened the seal, then stared down at it. The closely-written letter in its beautiful but aggresively-written hand was as impenetrable to her as the print of the book had been. "I'm very sorry," she replied softly, "But please advise His Grace that I cannot read French."

He stood, inclining his head. "I will do so at once." He hesitated, then said, "His Grace is a good man at heart. I hope he will soon understand that you will not judge him as others have."

"No, I swear it." She smiled a little. "Portman...thank you."

She felt a little better, enough to get some food in her stomach anyway. Nevertheless, sadness and apprehension still chewed at her as she settled in at her window seat to pen another letter to her father. How was she to fix this miscommunication with her new husband if he would not speak to her?

She had barely pulled out her writing set when she heard a door slam down the hall, and running feet. Before she could even set aside the wooden tray, she heard someone rapping urgently on the door.

She got up and hurried over, slippers shuffling against the wooden floor, and opened it. To her amazement, the Duke stood there, his chest heaving and her book gripped tightly in one hand.

Blinking rapidly, she pulled the door open and stepped back to let him in. He hesitated on the threshold, then stepped inside, shutting the door behind him. "A-am I to understand...." he had to stop and focus for a moment, the stutter threatening his every syllable in his agitation. "Am I to u-underst-stand that you do n-not read French?"

She took a deep breath, answering him as if she had not noticed the breaks in his speech. "Not a word of it, I'm afraid, My Lord. I fear that if you wish to correspond in writing, my languages do not include French. I decided on Latin instead, so that I could read the classics."

His eyebrows neared his hairline as she spoke. "B-but why then did you have t-this...?" he gestured with the book, and she just smiled.

"Well, my Lord, if you remember, we were held up that day by an accident in the street. A Frenchman came out of his carriage to shout at the carter who had caused the problem, and he dropped his book. I hadn't the chance to restore it to him, but we did rescue it from the street. It appeared to be a philosophy book, so I thought--"

He scoffed in amazement, eyes going wide. "You believed this to be a *philosophy* book? You really d-don't read any French, do you?" In his surprise he abandoned all formality—but his voice steadied as well.

"No, My Lord. Why do you ask?"

He led her over to the window seat and sat down with her, settling the book across his long thighs. "This a-author is one of the most infamous m...men alive in France today. This Marquis has been j-jailed for obscenity, sedition and w-worse. This book is...." his ears reddened. "When I thought y-you were reading *Philosophy in the Boudoir* for pleasure, and carrying it about in public, I had no idea w-what to think!"

Her eyes widened, and she stared at him in slightly embarrassed astonishment. "What manner of books does this reprobate write?"

He turned even redder and looked at the ceiling. She stared at him in confusion...and slowly the truth dawned on her.

Her jaw dropped, and she looked down at the book. "Am I to understand that that is a volume of--"

"It is a play, My Lady," he replied in an awkward voice, gripping the book as if it might jump off his lap and attack her. "And yes, it portrays quite an...impure tale, on subjects inappropriate for a lady's entertainment."

Emily blinked down at the book. And then shocked him completely—by bursting out laughing.

"A-are you to tell me that you've been holed up and refusing to talk to me for three days because you thought I had selected a volume of French pornography for my casual reading?" She couldn't help it. All the doubt, all the fear and confusion had happened because she had unwittingly rescued some Frenchman's naughty novel from the mud! She could have been mortified, but after everything, she was just too tired. So she laughed.

He stared at her in shock and mild disapproval. "It's n-not funny," he protested. But slowly, the shock gave way to a faint smile. "N-no, actually, it is hilarious."

They laughed, sitting there on that window seat, alone together for the first time. She kept giving in to fits of giggles, while he chuckled almost silently, hiding his smile in his fist. "I h-have never been happier to be wrong in m-my life," he admitted finally, his eyes twinkling with a warmth she had not seen before.

"I as well, My Lord. I thought for certain that you disliked me."

He gave her another shocked look. "D-disliked you? I couldn't!" At her surprise, he smiled a little shyly. "I have s-so many regrets about that day, when I couldn't sp-speak to you at our own wedding. Lest your father and the vicar know!

"I sh-should have written you sooner. I am only free to say all that I mean in my l-letters. Otherwise this stutter of mine ruins all. You can hear it now, that w-which I had hoped to hide." His embarrassment showed plain on his face, and she hastily gave him a smile.

"Please, my Lord, don't concern yourself with hiding such a small thing from me! I am not some cruel-hearted courtier looking to gain an advantage on you. I am your wife. And though we know little of each other yet, I do know that I would be a poor one if I judged my own husband on some trivial flaw in his speech." Daringly, she touched his arm, and felt a tremor go through him.

"You d-do not care?" Relief and astonishment broke over his fine features and lit his eyes. It was as if she had lifted a great burden from his shoulders. Perhaps she had.

"My Lord, I do not care if you speak to me with a stutter, as long as you don't leave me alone in silence again. All this time, I truly did think you despised me."

"I d-did not. I swear it." His narrow, long-fingered hand covered hers gently as it lay on her lap, and she felt his pulse beating fast in his slim fingertips. He seemed more relaxed...but squeezed her hand with a strange urgency, and ran his thumb from her palm to her wrist and back.

The strange little caress made her breath catch. "Please, my Lord, then, tell me what you did think, for I am left in mystery."

He drew a deep breath. "I never...I n-never resented marrying a st-stranger. It is merely expected. You...you know this. How it is for those in our p-position. But you are c-correct, that does not make it comfortable. But...when I saw y-you...it was *worse*."

"Worse?" She looked at him worriedly, and he just smiled.

"If you h-hadn't been so lovely and c-charming, I might not have worried so much what you thought of me. But even a Duke has a h-heart, my Lady. I would not have suffered your d-disdain."

Emily blushed enormously. "Oh. I—I see."

He took up the book again. "When I s-saw you with th-this, I...knew you were w-well read, but *this* book...the scandal if someone else had c-caught you with it...."

"I am sorry, my Lord. It was an honest mistake."

"I understand that now. But I w-wasn't certain what to do when I thought that...that...."

"That I would read pornography for entertainment, my Lord?" she tilted her head, looking down at the book. "What in the world is *in* that book?"

"It concerns the c-corruption of a young l-lady of quality," he murmured, and Emily was shocked to see a flush creep over his pale cheeks. His pale eyes swept over her briefly, and then he looked away out the window.

"And you read it?"

He nodded mutely, his mouth working. "I did not know w-what to think of the idea that you would be e-entertained by such decadence. But the thought of it...it occupied me. It stole my s-sleep."

Emily was young, and she was naïve in many ways, as she was slowly coming to learn. But there was a gleam in his eyes that sent shivers through her, and it reminded her again of that breathless infatuation of months that she had nurtured with just his portrait to gaze upon. "I know nothing of...such things," she murmured in response. But then her eyes searched his face, and she grew a little bold. "I do not know what is in that book, but I am certain it would be foreign to me. Unless you were so good as to teach me of it."

He drew a strange sort of shivery breath, and his hand slid up her arm and over her shoulder, and then into her hair. "I should call such writing an abominaton. But d-damn me, and damn its influence. Those sleepless nights were full of dreams of you regardless." Again his voice seemed to even out as passion and focus took it over. "The man in me sought to overrule the husband, and the Duke, and make a savage of me. I dreamt of c-corrupting you myself!"

She looked at him, and smiled gently, tilting her face up toward him in as much invitaton as she she dared. "You are my husband, my Lord. Would it truly be corrupting me to show me your desires?"

He stared at her for a long moment. Then he lunged toward her. She found herself crushed against him, bundled desperately against his chest as his mouth crashed down on hers. The feeling, the intimacy, after a lifetime without kisses, left her shaking and clinging to him.

Her heart pounded as she felt his hands start to roam over her through the pale muslin of her dress, and then start tugging and even tearing at the stays that kept it on her. His hands shook, and he made small sounds in his throat as his mouth ravaged hers, like a starving man with a feast laid suddenly before him. She froze for a moment, and then started helping her, slipping out of the dress and kicking off her shoes, then feeling him set to work on her petticoats.

Fear and doubt crumbled like dead leaves in a furnace, gone to ash in seconds as he carried her to her bed. *I will have to tell Annie that she was right,* she thought in dizzy amazement as he settled her half-dressed on the bed and started tugging off his own clothes.

He didn't leave room for her self-consciousness to take root. By the time her corset fell to the floor he had one of her nipples in his mouth, and she squirmed under him, gasping for air while he stripped off his waistcoat and shirt and then took hold of her again.

Annie had warned her that it would hurt when her husband came to her bed, at least the first few times. She hadn't been specific. Perhaps she had meant the ache that rose up in Emily now, like hunger pangs but centered lower, in that untouched place between her thighs. His touch filled her with warmth, and an unfamiliar pleasure that left her limp and panting with shock—but it stoked up that ache as well, until she trembled, barely able to bear it. When his roaming hands finally stripped her of the last scrap of cloth, and one wandered between her thighs, she gasped and squirmed, blushing furiously—only to fall back with a moan as his fingers started moving against her gently.

The motion of his hand between her legs drove her to a sort of madness, driving the pleasure and the ache up to greater and greater heights with each swirl of his fingertips. Her eyes closed; her back arched rhythmically, hips moving in response to his slow, lascivious caresses.

She heard a rustle of cloth and the thump of his house-shoes hitting the floor, and then he was clambering onto the bed with her. She dared open her eyes, and saw him staring down at her with a fevered, almost predatory gaze. Then his head dipped, and she felt something thicker than his fingers pressing against her.

He pushed into her, pain and pleasure mixing, his hand still moving tirelessly as she cried out and went rigid, overwhelmed with sensation. The ache and joy and craving all crested inside of her—and then relief washed over her in waves.

She collapsed under him even as he started to move his hips in the same convulsive way, his eyes closed and his face creased with tension. She watched, eyes dim and body deliciously relaxed, as he arched above her, panting for air as she had, trembling harder and harder as she had. And finally she understood, and held him, murmuring soft encouragement as his voice rose in little shouts of joy.

They lay there afterward, both a little stunned, their bodies limply entwined. Finally he took hold of the edge of the coverlet and folded it back over them for warmth. "I h-hope that I did not shock you," he murmured.

"Perhaps, My Lord, I do not mind when you shock me in such ways," she replied dizzily, her smile feeling sloppy on her lips.

He smiled, and went quiet for a little while.

She lay with her head on his shoulder, and finally ventured a little teasingly, "I am still curious as to what that book contains."

He opened an eye. "Ah, as your husband I should not in good conscience expose you to such filth, My Lady."

She pouted at him, and he chuckled and kissed her nose. "What will become of it now?"

"I shall see that it is properly disposed of, of course."

She looked him in the eye. He avoided her gaze for a moment, and she started giggling against his chest. "I think that perhaps my Lord intends to keep it."

His expression went mock-stern. "Now that would be absolutely improper of me! Where would you get that impression?"

"You read it, didn't you?"

He paused, blinking, and a brief, lopsided grin tugged at his lips. "Well yes, I might have. And perhaps I *am* keeping it, at that." He kissed the end of her nose.

I'm going to have to learn to read French, Emily thought. She drifted off in his arms, a mischievous smile still on her face.

*****

THE END

Enjoy what you read? Please keep flipping to the end of the book to leave a review on Amazon. Thanks!

Want to read HOT, NEW romance ebooks every week? Click HERE to sign-up and instantly Get news about my new and upcoming releases as well as special offers

Click here to return to the start of the book

Printed in Poland
by Amazon Fulfillment
Poland Sp. z o.o., Wrocław

54348633R00130